Ribbons
of the Sun

A Novel

Harriet Hamilton

Brown Barn Books
Weston, Connecticut

Brown Barn Books
A division of Pictures of Record, Inc.
119 Kettle Creek Road, Weston, CT 06883 U.S.A.
www.brownbarnbooks.com

RIBBONS OF THE SUN

Library of Congress Control Number 2006923182
ISBN: 0-9768126-2-2
978-09768126-2-3
Hamilton, Harriet
RIBBONS OF THE SUN

Printed in the United States of America

To those children of Mexico,
too many of whose lives are symbolized by
the fictional children in this book.
May they find their way home.

Acknowledgements

My deepest thanks to Nancy Hammerslough at Brown Barn Books for her insightful suggestions and great patience; to Michael Green, who saw merit in a hastily written first draft; to Darcy Pattison, who kept assuring me rewriting was just a matter of craft; to Karen Taha and Jan Van Schuyver for their encouragement; to the Reverend Delle McCormick, whom I met on the streets of San Cristobál; and especially to my Friend and the Ancestors, who wanted very much for this story to be written. I am most profoundly grateful.

Harriet Hamilton
Fayetteville, Arkansas
Fall 2005

Prologue

In my village we grow flowers. Big, strong, beautiful flowers. Carnations, roses, calla lilies, daisies—all kinds of flowers. When their buds start to open and they are the most beautiful, we take them to Santa María del Sol and sell them in the marketplace. My mother always told me I was her special flower, a gift from la Virgen. That's why she named me Rosa.

Chapter One

"That you, Rosa? Don't ask her again, child."

"No, Abuelita, I won't."

My grandmother seemed to have more eyes than a peacock. I put my schoolbooks on the table, left my shoes and socks by the door and spread my toes against the cool earthen floor.

A small white flower I picked on the way home made its way into the empty bottle in front of the picture of the Virgin. "It's your favorite color," I whispered to her, moving the small candle my mother kept burning to one side. "Please convince my papí to take me to the city."

I glanced quickly back at the other room. "But don't let my grandmother find out. It has to be our secret." I turned away from the small altar and leaned through the doorway that led to the other room. "Mmmm, Abuelita, the tortillas smell good today!"

My grandmother sat on the floor in front of the fire in the center of the cooking room. "Don't be asking her to let you go to the city," she called.

"No, Abuelita." What did she know, anyway? She was just an old woman.

"It's no place for young girls. I may be an old woman, but that much I know. There's no good that comes to a young girl in the city."

How did she always know what I was thinking?

In front of her, a flat round metal sheet balanced on three large stones, under which the god of fire, fed with twigs and small branches,

1

glowed orange and red. Dark gray smoke wafted up from underneath the comal, reaching freedom through the open windows. The walls, blackened by years of fires and tortillas, held the aroma of roasted corn.

My grandmother looked up, her hands never stopping. "Did you hear what I said?"

I giggled. "Abuelita, you're so silly. What do you know about the city? Have you ever been there?"

"I know that as long as I'm alive it will never come to that," she mumbled. "I'll make sure of it."

I didn't understand why she felt so determined to keep me from something so wonderful, but it did me no good to argue. I unbuttoned my school uniform, stepped out of it, hung it on a hook my father had put up and slipped my blouse over my head. I took a deep breath, of the smell I loved so much. "Did you put magic in the tortillas today?"

"What do you mean, niña?" My grandmother chortled. She reached under the dishcloth into the damp mound of dough beside her and pinched off a little piece. She rolled it into a ball with both hands and patted it out into a smooth, perfect circle, pausing just long enough to turn one tortilla over and take another off the comal. "Who put such an idea into your head?"

I reached for my black woolen skirt, the one my mother had made for my eleventh birthday. I held it briefly to my nose. Like Saint John the Baptist who lived in the sheep, these clothes were real. I took the belt my grandmother and I had woven together, wrapped it around the skirt at my waist and skipped into the cooking room. "Papí says the corn gives us life, but I know it's your magic that feed us."

"How would a girl no bigger than a chicken know that?"

I laughed and sat down next to her. She was round and soft like drops of liquid sunshine from the gods themselves. Her white hair hung in a long braid down the center of her back like silk hangs from the stalks of corn. Her plump hands patted out another round of dough. Her hands and the dough blended into each other, smelled like each other, molded each other. "Because I can taste it." I snuggled under her arm. "And I can feel it in you." I took a deep breath. "When will you teach me your magic?"

She reached out to take a tortilla off the comal and put another in its place. "Someday." She tucked the warm tortilla inside the folds of the dishcloth and hugged me close to her body.

I put my arms around her. "Oh, Abuelita, I can't wait that long. Can't you teach me now?"

My mother walked through the door carrying an armload of clothes, bleached by the sun god and stiffened by the god of the wind. "Rosa, have you fed your chickens yet?"

I pulled back and shrank into my grandmother's softness. I hadn't and my mother knew it. "Not yet, Mamá." I had named each chicken, which made me responsible for them. Two red ones, three white ones and one black one. My grandmother said those were the sacred colors of the earth.

"We only have six left—is it too much to ask you to take care of them? Where is your sense of honor?"

I played with the long braid that hung down my grandmother's back. "Six chickens are a lot of work."

"There's honor in work. If you don't feed them, they'll wander off or die and we'll have no more eggs." The sharp edges of her voice followed her into the other room. "Aren't we hungry all the time already? We've already lost so much. Do you want us to lose the eggs, too?" She piled the clothes in the other room and came back into the cooking room. "It's bad enough your father doesn't mend the fences to keep in the goats. He spends half the morning looking for them instead of working in the fields. No wonder we have nothing to eat."

I buried myself more deeply in my grandmother's arms. My mother's tone had become harsh of late.

My grandmother squeezed me. "It's an honorable thing to have a responsibility."

I looked up at her and smiled. "I know, Abuelita. Our people are responsible for remembering the saints, for keeping the sky in place with the World Tree, and for taking care of the gods."

"That's right." She leaned forward to turn another tortilla. "So having a responsibility means you are part of a great circle."

I hugged her. "Okay."

She whispered in my ear. "No more talk of going to the city."

"No, Abuelita." I looked away. I wouldn't talk about it, but I knew

I would still ask. It was my chance to show my family that I was responsible. I turned back to my grandmother. She knew about responsibility. She ground the corn, made the tortillas, and healed. She called the gods and said the prayers and put the person's sickness into the rooster. Then she snapped the rooster's neck and the person got well. She healed a lot of people like that. I went with her sometimes. "When I grow up I am going to heal people, like you."

She winked and patted out another round of dough. "You will. But for now, it's chickens."

My mother came in from the other room. "You can help me fold these after we eat."

"Yes, Mamá." My mother was round like my grandmother, but not as soft. She didn't have time to be soft. Her hair hung down her back in two braids, tied together with ribbons, just like mine. Her face looked as dry as the fields, and in some ways she seemed older than my grandmother.

"As soon as she has done her homework." My father stood outside the doorway, shaking the dust from his hat and stamping the dirt from his feet. "School is first."

"School. You think school is the answer to everything. School doesn't feed us." My mother frowned at my father and turned to stir a pot of beans that had been simmering from the night before. "Did you find something to mend the fence with?"

"Yes." My father stepped inside and wiped his brow with the back of his hand. "The sun is strong today."

"All you do is complain," my mother said, her back to him. "Soon enough the gods will send the rain and you will be saying it's too wet to work. Rain is good. We will have plenty of flowers to sell."

My father hung his hat on a peg by the door. "I don't complain. You always say I complain, but it's not complaining. It's these bones. They're too old to work so hard."

"There is harder work than selling flowers, Old Man."

My father rubbed the back of his neck. His gnarled brown hands were the same color as the earth. But the earth was soft and his hands were not. They were tough and scarred. "You talk as if it were up to me." He glanced at me with sad eyes and shook his head. "If things don't get better, we will have only one flower to sell."

I didn't know what he meant, but my mother whirled around, the spoon still in her hand. Her eyes flashed with fire. "Don't even think such a thing!"

That night I unbraided my grandmother's hair and brushed it with long smooth strokes. All the years of her life were in her hair. All her knowledge and all her goodness. I put the brush down and ran my fingers through her hair, wanting to hold her and her magic.

As if she knew the future, she half-turned to me and reached for my hand. "Rosa, you belong to your people—never forget."

I smiled and squeezed her hand. I knew who I was, where I had come from and who I belonged to. How could I forget? "No, Abuelita, I won't."

The next morning even before I opened my eyes, I knew. Against mine, my grandmother's body felt cold and empty. I pushed back the blankets, got up and backed away, horrified at what had happened while I slept.

My mother put her arm around my shoulder. "The old gods came for your abuelita while she was sleeping. It's easier that way."

I wrestled free of her embrace. "I don't think it's easier. I think it's cruel. What gods would take away the person you love the most?" I pulled away. "I don't need those gods."

"Child! Watch what you say!"

Later that morning my father made a pine box and my parents laid her body inside and placed it in the middle of the room. I stood to one side, watching, arms crossed. It was wrong, unfair. Spring was not supposed to bring death.

That afternoon the village elders came to sit with my grandmother and a shaman came from a nearby village to say the prayers. People from our village came in the evening. The shaman lit the candles, called the gods and prayed throughout the night. The smells of so many people, of incense, candle wax, flowers and aguardiente filled the house until there was no air left. I watched through the smoky haze as my parents inhaled death, filled their lungs with the possibility of death and embraced the inevitability of death. I could not. I would not.

The next morning the village elders, red-eyed and hung over after an all-night vigil, nailed the lid on the rough pine box, hoisted it onto their bony shoulders and carried it away. Old women, in dresses as black as crows, walked alongside, wailing and moaning over the box. Behind them, four slightly drunk musicians played loud and off-key all the way to the cemetery. Lots of people cried. It was good, for a funeral. She probably liked it. I didn't.

Above the cemetery the sun watched from the sky, watched as the men struggled against the wind to lower the pale rough-hewn box into the pale, roughly dug hole, watched as the dry earth swirled and fought against the box, watched as the fierce wind stole the words from the mouth of the priest.

I watched, too, as the men shoveled the lifeless dirt onto the box. I stooped down and picked up a handful of it. A part of me had been ripped out, like this narrow piece of earth.

Around me the air sizzled, crackled, sparked, threatened to catch on fire. I squeezed the dirt, determined not to cry. Then of its own accord my hand opened, and the dirt trickled out. Tears came. I turned away from the box and staggered into the wind, pushing against it as it tried to shove me back into the embrace of death.

I ran into the fields. My grandmother's death had ripped the masks off the faces of the gods, and now, for the first time, I saw them as they were—capricious and uncaring. I railed at the sky, at the mountains, at the sun itself. "This life is a lie! Everything we do is a lie!" I cried. "Our offerings are just bribes!" I shouted.

I raised my voice and shook my fist at the mountains. "We don't love you. We're afraid of you. Our prayers aren't love poems, they're to keep you away." I sobbed and lifted my fist to the heavens. "It's a lie, all of it." I threw myself against the ground. "I don't need you anymore."

This relationship between the gods and the people wasn't about love or honor or mutual responsibilities. It was about fear. My hands pounded the earth that my grandmother had called sacred. It wasn't sacred. It was the enemy, waiting with open jaws like the crocodile.

That awful day finally came to an end like all the others, when the Sun god slipped behind the mountains and made his descent into the Underworld. It was a day I would never forget.

The terrible thing about death is that life rushes in and surrounds it, filling in the empty space as though it had never existed. You were here and then you were gone and life went on without you. It didn't make sense. The week after my grandmother's funeral I went back to school. My teacher expected me to hand in my homework and my chickens expected their dinner.

Little by little I forgot the things I had said that terrible day and the betrayal I felt. In spite of my grandmother's warning, I continued my secret prayers to the Virgin. At home my mother made the tortillas, my father worked the fields and nobody made magic.

I filled the emptiness my grandmother had left with my best friend, Micaela. At school we shared the same desk and often did our homework together. She was taller than me and her mouth was wide and always laughing. Her teeth were bigger and her eyes more rounded. Everything about her was bigger and more alive—maybe that's why I liked being around her. She also thought everything was funny, and when we were together, it was.

"Bet you don't know what sound this letter makes," she said, giggling and pushing a hastily drawn "h" in front of me.

I turned the paper around, examining the letter from each of its four sides. "It depends on which way you look at it," I said.

She motioned for me to lean toward her. "Come here, I'll make the sound for you."

I put my ear next to hers but I didn't hear anything.

She laughed and pushed me away. "That's because the 'h' doesn't make any sound in Spanish."

"Then how can there be a letter if there is no sound for it?"

We laughed at the idea that someone somewhere in Spain had created a letter for which there was no sound. Our teacher didn't see the humor in it, but it seemed funny enough to us.

Sometimes we traded shoes just for fun. Her feet were bigger than mine and they didn't go all the way in, so she had to walk around on tiptoe. One day we traded uniforms and when I went home for lunch my mother kept looking and looking at me. "Rosa, you need to eat more," she said, handing me another tortilla. I stuffed a piece into my mouth and tried hard not to giggle.

Micaela and I made a pact to be best friends forever. "When you are a shamana, I will be your rooster," she said one day when we were playing in the river.

I laughed and shook my head. "No, you can't be my rooster. The rooster dies. You have to be something else."

"Then I'll be your saint. I'll wear a really big mirror so you can sit in my heart and I'll whisper your prayers to the gods."

I smiled. Maybe the saints could be trusted even if the gods couldn't. "That would be good. Just don't take too long."

While there were four of us it was easy to hold up the sky. It was only when we were three that everything came crashing down. The gods must have discovered that I no longer believed in them, because that summer they didn't send us any rain. My father had fewer and fewer flowers to take to market.

Each week the water in the river got lower, until soon there was hardly enough for our small garden or to drink. The water had so much dirt in it everything tasted gritty. We drank grit, we bathed in grit and we washed in grit. By mid-summer there wasn't even enough grit for the garden and our squash and tomato plants dried up. We went to bed with empty stomachs.

That September it rained, but I didn't go back to school. My father said there wasn't enough money for the uniform. Fall had arrived like an empty-handed guest.

"It's okay, Papí. None of my friends are going. They don't have enough money either."

He squatted down in front of me. "Then you're not upset?"

I caressed his cheek. "Ay, Papí, how could I be upset? Not with you—never." I put my arms around him and hugged his neck.

Even though I didn't go to school I still had plenty to do. Without my grandmother, we all had more responsibilities. First I had to feed my chickens. After their bellies were full I picked them up and held them and told them how beautiful they were. They reminded me of my grandmother, but then everything did. For her everything, every action, every person pulsed with life and glowed with purpose.

After I fed the chickens I had to carry water up from the river. It was easy, except for when Micaela and I giggled too much. Sometimes we splashed each other and had to go back and refill the buckets. Then we had to wait until our clothes dried, so our mothers wouldn't know what we had done. We'd sit on a large rock on the bank of the river and tell each other funny stories or ask unanswerable questions. Micaela was good at making up answers. She'd put on a serious face like the school-teacher and I'd never know whether it was the truth or not until she burst out laughing.

"What do you think the gods do for fun?" I asked.

She thought for a moment. "I think they like to go to the celebrations." She turned to me. "I think they love the fireworks and the banners and the music and the flowers—everybody does. I think they help us so that we will throw them parties."

I waited for her to laugh, but this time she was serious. I nodded. "Yes, I think you're right." The celebrations were the best times, even though they cost a lot of money. "They won't be expecting much of a party this year, surely, because they haven't done anything."

Micaela gave me a playful shove. "Silly! This year we have to give them an even bigger party, so they'll come back."

"Back? From where?"

She furrowed her brow. "Obviously they have found better parties in other villages. They're having such a good time they've forgotten about us. We have to get them back."

I nodded. So that's how it worked. "I see." Maybe my grandmother was having a good time, too. Maybe that's why they had come for her.

In spite of our plans to keep our splashing a secret, my mother seemed to know about each drop I lost on the way back. "Don't be so careless, Rosa. Water is life," she scolded.

I tried to make her understand it wasn't my fault. "I didn't mean to spill any, Mamá. The drops just jump out by themselves. Honest."

But my mother didn't see things that way. "You bring dishonor on the whole family when you don't do your part."

That winter my father got up earlier to work longer in the fields, but without rain it didn't really matter how well he tilled the soil or how affectionately he spoke to the flowers. One day he walked over the mountain to another village, but they were not much better off than we were. Another day he rode the bus into Santa María to look for work, but he said there was no work in the city for a man who only knew how to till the fields. He and my mother argued a lot; I don't know what about. They lowered their voices when I came into the room, and their angry words simmered into angry looks.

One evening when they weren't arguing, my mother rubbed my father's feet. She unbuckled his worn leather sandals, pulled them off and rested his feet on her knees. It was hard to tell his sandals from his feet. Both were tough and leathery and both were the color of dirt. "Things are going to get better in the spring, just have a little patience."

My father just stared at the wall and shook his head.

I could see the weariness in his face, but he just laughed and said his love was stronger than his body. I looked into his eyes, wanting so much to make his exhaustion worth something.

My mother pulled out a jar of ointment. "This will take away your tiredness."

He smiled.

She dabbed a little on his feet and began to rub. "I traded for some candles today. I'm going to light them and make a special petition to the Virgin. She hears what I say. You'll see."

My mother lit candles and said her special prayers, but nothing changed. The earth got drier, the river got lower and my parents got more and more worried.

In the winter afternoons my mother taught me how to transform colored thread into carnations and lilies and roses. One evening she showed my father a cloth I was embroidering. "Rosa and I are growing our own flowers," she announced. She tossed the cloth around her shoulders and danced across the room. "Soon we will have plenty of flowers to sell, even without rain."

And even if the gods don't come back, I added silently. I put my arms around my father's waist. "Papí, you and I can take these flowers into the city. We can sell them with your flowers, and then we'll have plenty to eat."

He smiled and tugged on my braids.

"Papí, you just have to give me a chance. People in the city have lots of money. They will buy my flowers, just like they buy yours. I'm sure of it."

But we didn't go to the city and no one came to our village to buy flowers. The ground was hard and cracked, and the spring winds, when they came, brought a dryness that stung our skin instead of the rain that would have brought us back to life. Maybe Micaela was right. The gods had found a better party.

I was folding clothes that day when my father came home from the fields early. From his hand a bunch of broken stalks dangled, the roots still attached. He shuffled into the house and dropped them onto the floor.

My mother looked up from the comal and stopped what she was doing. I stood in the doorway, afraid my father would break if I spoke. His shoulders drooped and his head hung down like he had given up. As though his bones had crumbled. I felt bad for him, bad that everything I had done had not been enough. He slumped down into the little chair across from where my mother had been patting out tortillas and stared into the embers. It was a long time before he said anything. Finally he wiped his eyes and looked up. "The goats broke through the fence. There's nothing left."

My mother stifled a cry. "The vegetable patch?"

"Everything is gone. Everything." My father leaned forward, rested his forehead against his fist and stared into the embers, his face dead, his voice monotone, his body limp.

"We still have some seeds."

He shook his head. "I traded them for corn."

"Then we have nothing." She glanced at the doorway where I stood and shook her head. "I won't..." She hesitated, lowering her voice. I didn't hear what she said; only the sadness with which she spoke.

My father grunted. "We've come to it."

My mother wiped her cheek. She murmured something and gave him a warm tortilla. "Perhaps some special prayers by the priest."

But my father only shook his head. "Those saints don't know how to call the rain. They never have." He tossed the tortilla back onto the comal and turned around to the doorway where I stood. "Rosa, this

11

afternoon you must get your belongings together. Tomorrow morning you and I will go into the city."

My heart jumped in my chest. "Oh, Papí, thank you!" The city! My prayers to the Virgin had been answered. I dashed toward him and threw my arms around his shoulders. "At last you are going to take me with you to the market. I will be a big help, Papí, I promise."

My father didn't return my embrace. He just hung his head and stared at the floor.

My mother stared numbly into the fire. I pulled back from my father's shoulders and tugged playfully on his shirt. "It'll be all right. You'll see, Papí."

He kicked the embers, pushed the chair back and rushed out of the house. In the other room the candle on the altar flickered and went out.

Chapter Two

My mother was unusually quiet the next morning. She sat before the fire and stirred the glowing embers absently with a stick. Outside a million stars twinkled in the heavens.

"I wish you were coming with us, Mamá. It'll be such fun!" I shivered, partly from the chill of the morning and partly from the excitement.

She glanced up from the cooking fire and handed me a stack of warm tortillas wrapped in a cloth.

"I'll tell you everything as soon as we get back." I hugged my mother, kissed her cheeks and picked up the small plastic bag that held my embroidered flowers.

My mother took the bag and added a comb, a picture of the Virgin and a candle. "Just to be sure."

I didn't know why she thought we would need them, but I took them anyway and my father and I set out in the dark toward the mountain. He slung a bag over his shoulder, but it didn't seem to have much in it. Certainly no flowers. He didn't explain and I didn't ask. The next village was at the base of the other side of the mountain. It was a long walk. My father had walked the path many times and knew the way even in the dark.

My father didn't say much that day. He wasn't much of a talker anyway, but since it was my first trip, I thought he would tell me about everything we passed, just the way he explained everything about the festivals. Maybe he was thinking about what he would sell in the market. By the time we arrived at the bus terminal, long purple shadows snaked their way across the thirsty earth. I stood beside my father as he bought two tickets.

We sat down on the curb to eat the tortillas my mother had packed for us and to watch the sun come over the mountain.

"Papí, isn't today the most beautiful day you can imagine?"

He stared ahead, chewing slowly on a bit of tortilla.

I took a deep breath. The sky was changing from deep purple to that kind of blue you can fall into forever. The air was crisp and not yet too dry. The sounds of sheep bleating, the clacking of their hooves on the cobblestones, the smells of chocolate and coffee and fresh bread—life was so full, so rich—it somehow seemed impossible that it had left us out.

"Third class for Santa María!"

My father stood up and motioned for me to follow. "Let's go."

I clamored onto the big metal bus and followed him midway down the narrow aisle. He stopped and gestured with his hand. "Here. Sit there, next to the window."

I slid in across a brown seat with a big tear across the middle of it. He took hold of the round metal bar that divided us from the seat in front and slumped down next to me.

Outside my window people arrived with burlap sacks squawking with chickens and bulging with produce and flowers. On top of the bus, men yelled and waved their arms. After a lot of pushing and pulling and shouting, the burlap sacks were firmly tied to the rungs on the top of the bus. I knelt sideways on the seat and leaned toward my father. "Is the bus always this exciting?"

He mumbled something and adjusted his hat.

I gave him a kiss on the cheek. "I'm so glad we're going together. When I learn my way around, I can go by myself and you can stay home and rest."

My father stared ahead with a blank expression on his face.

"Isn't that so, Papí?" I put my face in his, breaking his daydreams.

He nodded and brushed me aside. "I wish it were so, hijita."

I opened my bag and peered at my embroidered cloth. "I wonder how much this will bring in the market."

My father didn't answer.

"Do you know how much, Papí?"

He shook his head.

"Well, I think it will bring us a good price!" I turned around and looked at the rows of seats behind us. People talked, others pulled food out of pockets or bags; still others closed their eyes and leaned against the windows. The bus bulged, overflowed with life and movement. It was glorious. Each of us had a dream and each of us was going to Santa María, the city that fulfilled wishes. I wanted to remember every detail so I could describe it to my mother tonight, and to Micaela tomorrow.

Two men talked by the door. What was taking so long? Didn't they know my life was finally about to begin? At long last one of them turned and climbed on board and started the motor. He may as well have started my heart. I turned to my father with a big smile. "Oh, Papí, this is the beginning of wonderful times; I can feel it in my heart."

He gave me a tight-lipped smile and stared ahead.

"Papí, I will make you proud of me, I promise. You and Mamá won't have to argue anymore. You'll see. My flowers will bring us plenty of money."

He seemed almost not to hear me. "Papí, are you angry with me?"

Tears filled his eyes. "No, hijita, no. Don't ever think that."

The bus left the village and wound through the mountains. The wheels of the bus turned on the rim of the steep drop just outside my window. I leaned forward in my seat when the bus strained to climb the steep hills and then peeked through my fingers when it careened slightly out of control, brakes squealing, down the other side. We were covered in dust in no time, but it was new dust, different dust, exciting dust.

In Santa María we got off the bus and walked to the market. If the village was full of life, the city was a hundred times fuller. A hundred times more exciting. Everywhere we walked was full of noise and color and movement. My grandmother said life was movement. If that was true, then I was truly alive in this moment. The air smelled of wet sidewalks and fresh bread and exhaust fumes. Above us the trees greeted the day with the raucous chatter and squabble of a thousand birds, while all around us the streets swelled with the voices and movements of throngs of people. I squeezed my father's hand. "This is truly paradise, Papá!"

We walked hand in hand on the sidewalk. Buses and cars roared past us in the streets, disappearing behind clouds of black smoke. And for anything you wanted to buy, there was a shop.

"Papí, look!" I broke away from his hand and pressed my face to the store window. Bags and ropes and buckets and colorful trinkets my mother would love to have. I turned around. "Papá, can we stop here and buy something for Mamá?"

He pulled me away from the window. "We have to do what we came for, *niña*." Sometimes he still called me niña.

I laughed. "Papí, you silly. Have you forgotten I turned twelve last week? I'm not a little girl anymore. Now I'm your helper." The very thought sent chills of excitement down my spine and made my knees weak.

We crossed the street and entered the market. My eyes were barely big enough to see it all. So many colors, shapes, and smells. Round red tomatoes, long green chili peppers, huge burlap bags of brown coffee beans that glittered in the sunlight, mounds of bright yellow mangos, deep green nopales. There seemed to be no end to the wealth that lay before us. "Papí, why have you kept this a secret?"

He led me through the narrow aisles of the market, past stands of raw meat, stands hung with plastic market bags in every color and size, stands piled high with new molcajetes that hadn't yet been flavored with the spices they would someday grind, and stands glistening with shiny new machetes, itching as I was, to get to work. The excitement of roasting coffee beans, the comfort of fresh bread and the sweetness of freshly sliced fruit filled the air. This was life at its fullest. Why had my grandmother insisted the city wasn't a place for girls? Why had she told me not to pray for it?

I stood beside my father while he talked to a man. The man looked at me and shook his head, but my father put his arms on my shoulders and told him I was strong.

I smiled shyly and nodded, not sure why this stranger needed to know that.

The man pointed, gave him directions and we left. For a long time we walked.

"Are we going to sell my flowers in a shop, Papí?" I reached for his hand. His hands were rough and calloused, but to me they were the dearest hands in the whole world.

He grunted a reply I didn't understand.

Finally we stood in front of a wooden door of a big house. My father knocked and a lady in a dress and high-heeled shoes came to the door. She was the señora, the patrona. She nodded, looked at me, held my chin and studied my face. Her nails were long and painted dark red. On her arm she wore a shiny gold bracelet. Her skin was not the color of the earth. It was lighter, the color of my grandmother's casket. She smelled of perfume and her face was painted.

"So, girl, what can you do? Can you make the beds and clean the bathrooms and sweep?"

I nodded, for that is what my father had told me to do, even if I didn't understand everything she said. I didn't. I was just beginning to learn Spanish.

She turned to my father. "Can she wash clothes? Mop floors? Clean the kitchen?" My father nodded and smiled. I could tell he was proud of me. But why was he telling this woman who was a stranger to us both? It made no sense. They talked about money but he never showed her my flowers.

The woman looked at me again and let go of my chin. Her bracelet slipped down to her wrist. "Okay then, I'll give her a try." She turned to my father. "You come back in two weeks and I'll let you know if I'll keep her or not."

My father bowed lots of little bows to her and backed away. He rested his hand lightly on my shoulder. "Do what the patrona tells you."

I didn't understand. "What do you mean, Papí?"

"You're staying here." He turned and walked quickly away.

Stunned, I called after him. "I'm staying here?" My voice reached out to him, louder and higher pitched. "Without you, Papí?" My legs felt heavy, my stomach hurt. My hand reached out to stop him. "Wait, Papí! Wait! Where are you going?"

My father kept walking.

"Papí!" I called. "Wait for me! Don't leave me here!"

My father's figure grew smaller and his loping stride began to blend in to the sidewalk. A feeling of panic struck me. What was I supposed to do here? Why hadn't he shown the señora my flowers?

"Papí!" I strained on tiptoe to see through the tears that blurred my vision. What had just happened? Why had he left me here with this señora neither of us knew? Why wouldn't he explain it to me? "When are you coming back for me, Papí?" I cried hoarsely.

He walked straight ahead, turned the corner and disappeared. A feeling of numbness overtook me. Nothing seemed real. This wasn't happening. It made no sense.

The señora took me by the arm. "Come on now, girl. He's gone. You'll see him when he comes for the money." She went inside and I followed. "Pay attention to what I show you. This is the living room," she said.

I walked behind her, a jumble of feelings running through me. Why had my father left me here? She had said two weeks. Is that how long I would be here? I couldn't think. I didn't know what to think. A man with a puffy red face glanced up from reading the newspaper. He looked at me as if I were a mound of fruit in the market. I didn't like him.

"This is my husband, the patrón," the señora said. "You'll do as he says."

A look of satisfaction passed over his face, as if he had just bought and paid for me.

I looked away.

The señora walked on. "Here is the dining room." She opened a swinging door. "And this is the kitchen."

She led me through the kitchen. "This is your room—in the back."

My eyes opened wide—my room? In my house we only had two rooms. A gasp of surprise flew out of my mouth. The room had a real bed. Our teacher had told us they had beds in the city, but Micaela and I thought she was making it up. A real bed, not a straw-filled mat on the floor. Next to it a small table and a closet. For two weeks I was going to sleep on a real bed. And then I would go home and have lots to tell.

She pointed. "Leave your things here and come into the kitchen."

I put the plastic bag with my embroidery on the bed and looked around. Two weeks wouldn't be so bad. My stomach clenched. As long as I stayed away from the man behind the newspaper.

She walked out into the kitchen. "This is Doña Elvira," the señora said. "She'll tell you what to do." Then she walked through a swinging door and left us alone. Orange and blue tiles climbed the walls. A big sink sat up against one wall, and across from it was the biggest cooking fire I had ever seen. The tongue of the god of fire flickered through the holes in the top.

Doña Elvira put her hands on her hips. "Have you ever worked before, girl?" Her voice was shrill and her eyes were hard, as if they had seen too much.

"No."

She turned toward the stove. "Well, you'd better learn quickly. I have enough to do around here without having to teach you."

I stood, unsure of what to do.

"Go put on a uniform and get to work! And wash your hands and face—you're full of grit. Just came in on the bus, no doubt." She pointed toward my room with the wooden spoon in her hand.

When I didn't move right away she threw down the wooden spoon, grabbed me by the arm and marched me to the room where I was to sleep. She yanked open the cupboard she called an armoire and pulled out a dress. "Here, put this on, clean yourself up and report back to me. At once!"

I took the dress from her and she marched out with the same hurry she had marched in. I looked at the dress. It had little squares. That was good. My grandmother said the square represented the four corners of the earth and the four guardians that held it up. Now they would be my guardians.

I unwound the belt my grandmother and I had woven when I was six years old. I ran my fingers across the threads. They were like my grandmother's words. She said weaving cloth was like making a life. One thread at a time, one color at a time, and then it was complete. I didn't want to finish the belt. I wanted to go on weaving her words and my life together forever.

"Girl! Hurry it up!"

I turned back to the narrow cot; slipped off the black woolen skirt my mother had made for my eleventh birthday and folded it carefully. In my village we all wore skirts like mine. They were gifts of Saint John the Baptist. He came with the priest's god, but he liked our village so much he decided to stay. He lived in the sheep; that's why we never ate them. We took their wool, but we would never have eaten their meat. Our skirts lasted for a long, long time, no matter if you grew or not. I held the skirt to my nose and took a deep breath. "Saint John the Baptist, I wish you were here with me."

"Girl!" Doña Elvira's face was inches away from mine. "Why are you standing in the middle of the room?"

I lowered my eyes to the floor. "I don't want to stay here. I want to go home."

Her face turned shades of red. "I'll have none of that in this house. You'll do as I say or you'll be out on the street." She turned and stormed out. "You'll wish you were dead rather than on the street."

My shoulders hunched up like they wanted to protect me. "I'll be right there."

I pulled my blue blouse over my head and folded it so as not to wrinkle the ribbons. My mother had shown me how to sew the ribbons on the seams. My blouse was blue, my favorite color in the whole world. It reminded me of the sky. That's the way I felt when I wore my blouse. Like there was a space inside me that went on forever.

The uniform felt flimsy after my real clothes. It felt almost like I wasn't wearing anything at all. I buttoned it all the way down and smoothed out the skirt. Then I went into the kitchen.

"Look at you! Didn't I tell you to wash up?" Doña Elvira's glance fell to my feet. "And put on your shoes!"

I didn't understand her. She grabbed me by the arm and led me to a little room that had water in it. She turned the faucet and water spurted out of the wall. I bent down and looked up into the spigot. "Is this where the god of water lives?" I asked.

My question only seemed to make her angrier. "This is a sink, stupid girl! It's to wash your hands. Here's the commode," she said, pointing.

I looked at the strange seat with a hole in the middle. I leaned over and jumped back. It was full of water.

Doña Elvira half-closed her eyes and shook her head. Before I could do anything at all, she lifted her dress and pulled down her panties and sat down on it. I stared, wondering how I would pull her out when she fell in. To my surprise she peed and then reached up and pulled a cord that sent water flushing down into the seat. I thought for sure she would be swept away by the force of the water. It had happened once in our village when the river flooded its banks. A boy had been swept away. No one ever saw him again. The gods of the water must have really needed him. They went to so much trouble.

Doña Elvira stood up, pulled her panties up and her skirt down. I stared. "Now do you understand?"

No, I didn't. I had never seen such a thing, not even in the books at school, but I nodded and said I did.

She turned on the faucet over the sink and handed me a towel. "Wash your face and hands. Today is Saturday and the guests will be here soon." She stormed out, mumbling to herself.

I wondered if my grandmother knew the gods of water lived in the walls. If there were walls like this in our village, we wouldn't have so many problems. I turned the faucet to make the water stop and then turned it again to make it flow. I had thought only my grandmother knew magic, but the city had its own kind of magic. Maybe that's why she didn't want me to come. The gods here were different. Maybe she thought I'd like them better.

"Girl!" I didn't need to see her face to know that she was still angry. I wondered if that's the way she always felt. What a waste of a good life to spend it in anger.

Now suffering, that was a different matter. At least according to the priest. He said if we suffered here we would be happy when we got to heaven. Maybe that's why my grandmother had gone with the old gods instead. Maybe she hadn't suffered and the priest's god didn't want her. The old gods didn't require suffering, although I did hear her say once that if you suffered in this lifetime, then the next lifetime would be easier. Maybe that's why the people in my village grew flowers—because we had already finished all the suffering that was required.

"Are you finished? Put on your shoes!"

I looked down at my feet. "I don't have any shoes," I called. "I don't go to school anymore. We sold my shoes."

She came to the doorway with a horrified look. "No shoes? The patrona is not going to like this. I hope she doesn't throw you out. Do

Chapter Three

I washed dishes until late that night. The guests in the other room seemed to be having a good time, but I was glad when they finally left. The next morning, Doña Elvira prepared to take her day off. "You'll wash up these dishes and clean the bathrooms," she said. "Make sure the living room is clean. The patrones will be leaving in a while and so will I. You will have the day to yourself. Make sure you make good use of it."

I nodded, afraid to ask questions and afraid I'd get in trouble for not doing everything I was supposed to.

"Don't forget to water the plants on the patio."

"No, I won't." A smile crept across my face. If only Micaela had come with me.

"And don't waste water!" She sounded like my mother when she was angry with me.

"No."

Sunday was a long day. I went up to the rooftop after everyone had left and I had finished my work. From up there I could see the whole city. It was a wonderful city. In the distance I could hear music and the noise of buses. I wondered what the people were doing on such a day. I wondered if they were on the streets like yesterday, or if they were spending the day with their families. I stayed up there for a long time, looking at the mountains and wondering which way was home.

Home! The very word filled me with happiness. I would have so many stories to tell—but more than that, I would be with the people I loved. To touch the earth with my feet, to fill my lungs with the crisp mountain air and hear the bleating of the sheep and goats—home—everything I loved and more. It was who I was, who my ancestors were. It was all of us, bound up together.

It was dark by the time the patrones returned. Later, after they had eaten and I had finished washing up, Doña Elvira and I sat down and drank hot chocolate she had brought from her village. She wasn't as mean as she had been the day before. Maybe my two weeks wouldn't be so bad after all.

I wanted to please Doña Elvira so she wouldn't be angry. The next morning I cleared the breakfast dishes without her having to tell me. I put them in the sink and began to wash them. I looked up when I sensed her standing over my shoulder.

"What are you doing, girl? Hurry up with those dishes. I have to go to the market and there's a lot of work still to do!" Then she turned away and muttered something like, "You are such a slow learner!"

The kitchen door swung open and the señora walked in. She glanced at me and handed Doña Elvira a wad of bills. "Take this girl to the market with you and get her some shoes, for God's sake!"

Two trips to the market in as many days was more than I had ever hoped for. Already I loved the smells, the narrow, damp passageways, buyers filling their shopping bags and the people tending the stands. It was too wonderful. So why had my grandmother been so against it?

I trotted along behind Doña Elvira, trying hard to keep up. She knew exactly where to go for the best shoes. We didn't go into the market, but instead went to a street nearby. We passed several stores when she turned and motioned for me to follow her into a doorway nearly hidden by all sorts of things—rope, rubber hoses, mirrors, blouses and more. We walked inside, past the buckets, tools and brooms to the back of the store. There before me lay more shoes than I had ever seen scattered every which way on shelves, dangling in pairs from ties and peeking out with more curiosity than my own from behind boxes.

Shoes! Who ever dreamed of so many shoes! Black ones and red ones, shiny ones and dull ones, tiny ones for babies and huge ones that only giants could wear. Shoes that, when you looked at them, you knew who would buy them—school shoes and working shoes, shoes that called feet to dance and shoes to walk quietly on stone floors. They were more than something to cover your feet—they were a call to identity. "Who are you?" they seemed to whisper. "What are your dreams? Where do you want to go?"

Pink bubbles of joy filled me as the possibilities of my life lined up, waiting for me to choose. They filled my face, put a blush of color in my cheeks, weakened my knees and made my feet tingle. My eyes roamed the shelves, wanting to take them all—wanting that pair for Micaela and this pair for Mamá and the ones in the corner—wouldn't they be perfect for Papí! I made up my mind to come back and buy them as soon as the señora had paid me. I never imagined how much joy shoes could bring!

Doña Elvira waited. Then her patience reached an end. "Pick out the ones you want, girl. We still have plenty to do."

I reached out toward the pair I knew I had to have. "These are the ones I want," I said.

Doña Elvira nodded, turned away and paid for them. When she had finished I was still holding them in my hands. The plastic was smooth and clean, and inside its pink walls were hundreds of tiny colored sparkles, like sunlight itself. I ran my fingers over them again and again. These shoes were magic—I knew they were. Together we would go on a magic journey and everything would be wonderful. My heart pounded with anticipation of what lay ahead.

"Well, don't just stand there, put them on."

I could hardly believe these magic shoes were mine! I bent down and put first one and then the other on, amazed at the way my feet sparkled through the clear plastic. "Look, Doña Elvira, aren't these the most wonderful shoes ever? They make my toes twinkle. Aren't they the most beautiful shoes you have ever seen?"

She smiled, half-closing her eyes and shook her head. "You are such a child."

But I knew she secretly liked them as much as I did.

Sometimes when Doña Elvira looked at me I had the feeling she was seeing someone else. That afternoon while we were eating her voice softened and she smiled when she spoke to me. "You are such a sweet girl. It's too bad you had to leave home."

I scooped a spoonful of soup. "I don't mind. I like helping my parents. It's my responsibility."

She nodded, broke apart a roll and dipped it into the hot, pasta-filled broth. "Are they old?"

I scraped the bottom of my bowl. The soup was good and I welcomed it on such a chilly day. "I think so. They are tired all the time. And the gods don't send any rain."

She nodded. "They must miss you very much."

I exchanged my empty bowl for a plate of food. "Yes, they love me very much."

Suddenly I wasn't who she thought I was and her tone changed without warning. "Stupid girl! Watch what you are doing. You almost broke that." She slapped my hand away from the plate. "You are so clumsy. You'll never be good for anything. You might as well leave before the señora fires you. She will, you know."

When she talked to me that way I felt confused. It seemed like I was two different people—one she liked and another she didn't. I never knew which one she was seeing.

I didn't know which one I was either. In my house I knew who I was, but in the señora's house everything was different. It was an unsettling feeling. Nothing, not even the clothes here had meaning. My uniform was thin and had none of my grandmother in it, none of my people and nothing of the ancestors. It was just a flimsy piece of cloth, not nearly strong enough to keep me safe.

The next morning Doña Elvira woke up in a good mood. "I'm going to teach you how to do lots of things in the kitchen," she said as we were finishing our breakfast. "You'll be a real cook when you leave here."

I smiled. "I hope so. I'd like to be a cook." I washed the dishes and went up to clean the bathrooms. When I came down, she was in the kitchen with her apron on.

"Today I'm going to prepare chiles rellenos," she said, handing me an onion. "Chop this and don't cut yourself."

I put the onion on a cutting board and began to cut. "Is that a special dish? My mother makes special food for the festivals." I looked up.

"Does your village have festivals? I like the fireworks best."

She snatched the knife from my hand. "No, no, that's all wrong. Didn't your mother teach you anything?" She cut the onion in half, then scored it with the knife and cut slices. "Do it like this." Little pieces, all perfectly square, fell as if by magic.

I took the knife and began to cut the way she showed me. "My grandmother always put magic in the food."

"Is that so?" She put the tomatoes on the open fire to loosen their peel and put the chiles she had toasted in a plastic bag.

I wondered if she knew how to make magic, but she didn't volunteer any information. "When I grow up I'm going to be healer like my grandmother." I lined up the knife and carefully cut through the onion.

Doña Elvira took the chiles out of the bag and began to peel them. The odor filled the kitchen and I took a deep breath. It was delicious already.

I was nearly finished with the onion and all my squares were almost as perfect as hers. I showed them to her. "I'm going to heal people the way she did." A heavy feeling settled in the pit of my stomach. The gods had left us. And maybe I had left them. No one could be a healer without the help of the gods. I shrugged. Maybe by then I would know the city gods.

"You'll be good at it, too. I always knew you were smart. I knew it from the first moment you were born." She stopped abruptly and turned away. Then she came back and began cutting again. "You're not smart. You're stupid. You can't do anything right." She went to the sink and rinsed her hands. " Look at the mess you've made with that onion. It's a good thing you don't serve the patrones their meals. You'd probably spill the food all over the floor. I don't intend to lose my job on your account."

I looked down at my onion. It didn't seem like a mess to me. Little squares in a neat pile. Wasn't that what she had shown me? I was glad I didn't serve the patrones their meals either, but for a different reason. I didn't like the patrón. The way he looked at me.

I had been here four days. My father would be coming for me soon and I could forget about the patrón and the way he stared. I would wear my magic shoes back to the shoe store, buy the bright red ones for

Micaela and the boots for Papí and the shiny white ones for my mother. Then we would get on the bus and go home.

"Pay attention! This is no time to daydream, girl!"

Doña Elvira's words jerked me back to reality. I watched as she poured oil into a big earthenware casserole and set it on the stove. "You'll have to do this by yourself someday." She pulled a package of ground meat out of the market bag. "Take the tomatoes off the fire. Take care you don't burn yourself. Then take out three eggs for the batter."

I did as she said and the kitchen soon filled with sweet and pungent aromas. My mouth watered and my stomach tied itself into a knot, remembering the days when smells were the only food it had.

That afternoon after dinner, Doña Elvira brought a stack of dishes back on a tray. She left them by the sink. "You wash up these dishes while I make the coffee. Then you and I will eat."

Doña Elvira opened the paper bag and poured the ground beans into the pot, filling the whole kitchen with the aroma. Her body was round like my grandmother's, but she wasn't at all like my grandmother. There was no softness in her. Her hair was short like a man's. It looked nothing like cornsilk. Her face was flat as if life had worn it down. Thick stubby fingers arranged blue and white cups, saucers and a sugar bowl on the tray, poured the hot coffee and carried it into the dining room. I was almost finished with the dishes by the time we sat down to eat.

We ate at a little table by the window. The table was painted red and had flowers around the rim. There were flowers outside on the patio too. Maybe I had been too quick to judge. It wasn't all bad in this place. There was more food than I had ever eaten in my life, and the work wasn't difficult. I hadn't had time to embroider any flowers, but as I worked faster, perhaps I would have time. My father would be here in another ten days, and I had to have flowers for him to sell.

"What's the matter, why are you picking at your food, girl?" Doña Elvira rested her fists on the edge of the table and leaned across.

I rubbed my stomach. "This is more food than I have ever eaten. When my papí comes I will be so big, he won't recognize me." I put my hand over my mouth and giggled. "We'd better make sure he doesn't take you home instead of me."

Doña Elvira giggled too. "Wouldn't he be surprised?" She was beginning to like me. Maybe she'd think of me like a daughter. That would be good. Then I wouldn't feel alone.

The next afternoon Doña Elvira went out on an errand. I was still in the kitchen, washing the dishes. In the living room the patrón and the señora yelled at each other. I could hear things breaking in there.

I was still standing at the sink when the patrón burst into the kitchen. His face was red. The veins in his neck stood out, big and purple. His breathing was heavy and his eyes were so big, I thought they were about to burst. A black angry cloud hung all around him. It scared me. He stared for a moment, turned around and stormed out. My whole body shook.

A moment later the front door slammed and the señora started to cry. I looked down at my magic shoes. Take me away from here, I whispered silently. Take me home. But my feet stayed put in front of the sink.

By the time Doña Elvira came back and I had bathed and put on my real clothes, the sky had turned shades of turquoise and green. I didn't know where to go, nor did I have any money, so it didn't really matter. I just wanted to be out of that house. I wiped my magic shoes off with a damp cloth. They sparkled and seemed to say "Let's go explore! Let's find something fun!"

I didn't know where to go, but my magic shoes knew exactly where they wanted to take me that day. We giggled as we danced along the sidewalk, stopping awkwardly at curbs and making funny plopping noises against the pavement.

The orange glow in the sky soon turned to purple and my shoes and I traveled from streetlight to store light, where they would magically light up and sparkle again. Darkness changed the things in the shops, too. I think they became alive. They pressed against the window and called out, "Where are you going? What are you going to do?" I smiled and glanced down at my magic shoes. Where were we going?

There were few places we didn't go. We walked through aromas of freshly grilled meats and warm tortillas. We walked through the sounds of laughter and clinking glasses. We walked through the noisy river of cars, tooting their horns and squealing to a stop. We walked through a quiet park where couples held hands and looked into each other's eyes. We walked through music and fresh bread and elote vendors and people hurrying home. We walked past shops as their metal gates crashed down and shopkeepers locked up for the night. My magic shoes made me feel safe. I was exploring on my own—something I would never have dreamed of doing before, and I was proud of myself. When my father came to get me, he would hardly recognize me, I would have grown up so much. I could hardly wait to show him.

That evening when I returned, Doña Elvira was making little sobbing noises in her room. I tiptoed to her door and peeked through the opening. She was sitting on her bed and rocking back and forth, holding something against her chest. She didn't see me and I didn't stay there very long.

The next day I stayed in the kitchen and then went up to the rooftop to wash clothes until the patrón left. Even when he didn't yell, he looked like a mountain that was ready to explode. I had never seen so much anger and it frightened me. That afternoon I didn't hear him come into the kitchen, and before I realized he was there, he was standing beside me, reaching across my body toward the cabinet. His hand brushed against me and I moved back, embarrassed.

"I need a glass."

I pulled away and tried to make myself small.

He pulled me back to where I had been standing and ran his hand across my body. "No, you're okay. Stay where you are."

I froze like an animal in a hunter's sights.

Later that day when I was finishing the dishes I told Doña Elvira I didn't like him.

"He's a very important person in the government, you know. You have to treat him with respect. That's what he wants, respect."

I would try to remember that. "How much longer until my father comes?"

"Soon enough, girl." She picked up a towel and began drying the glasses. "In the meantime, be sure you do everything the way the patrón likes it."

"Day after tomorrow is Saturday. So eight more days after tomorrow." I rinsed the last pot and reached for a towel. "I don't think the patrón is angry because of me. Yesterday while you were out they argued and the señora cried."

"What a gossipmonger you are!"

I shook my head. "I heard them."

Doña Elvira dropped the towel and slapped my cheek. "Well, quit listening!" She put her hands on her hips and glared. "And don't you repeat anything you see or hear in this house. What goes on here is nobody's business. You'll get us both fired. Do you know what happens to girls out on the street?"

I didn't, but from the tone of her voice, it wouldn't be good. After that I didn't tell her when they argued, even though I still heard them— the shouting, then the slamming doors, crashes and her crying. One day he brought her flowers. She threw them in the trash. I don't think she even noticed how beautiful they were.

In the kitchen Doña Elvira complained there wasn't enough to buy what she needed from the market and we ate chilaquiles made from stale tortillas. "There's never any money in this household. What do they expect me to do, produce a miracle? How can I prepare a meal if there is nothing to buy it with?"

It was okay with me. She made good chilaquiles—with onions and chicken broth and cheese. But it wasn't okay with the señor. He wanted meat. I think that was the problem. Not enough meat.

Finally it was Saturday again and a lot of their friends came to eat. The patrón had money today and it seemed he didn't mind spending it. I liked Saturday because the patrón was too busy to come into the kitchen and stare at me. He was too busy to reach past me for something and run his hand across my body.

One more week and my father would come for me and then there would be no more patrón. I would not tell my father the way the patrón looked at me or the way he brushed against me or how sweaty his hands were or how bad his breath smelled. I would not dishonor my father with city gossip.

Instead I would tell my father all the wonderful things I had learned about in the city. I would show him my new plastic shoes, all sparkly and shiny, and I would tell him how it felt to sleep in a real bed and how much food we had to eat.

That's what I thought about for seven whole days. Saturday finally arrived. As soon as I heard my father's voice at the door, I ran to get my things.

Doña Elvira blocked the doorway. "Not so fast, girl. You'll have plenty of time to talk to your father. The bathrooms have to be cleaned first."

"Now?"

She stood like a fortress, hands on her hips.

I grabbed the bucket and rushed up the stairs. I cleaned them as fast as I could and raced back down the stairs and into the kitchen. "Where is he?" I said, slightly out of breath.

She shook her head. "He waited for you, but you took too long. He said he had to leave." She turned the poblanos on the flame with a long pair of tongs. "I've been telling you not to dawdle."

"But I didn't." The bucket suddenly felt very heavy. "He left? Without me?" My arms sagged. "Is he coming back?" I set the bucket down.

She shrugged. "He didn't say." She took a chili pepper off the flame, put it into a plastic bag and turned a second one. "The señora told him you were a slow learner and that she could only pay half of what he expected."

I stared. He left me? How could he? "Did he say anything? A message for me?"

"He looked disappointed, but he took the money and left."

I fought back the tears. "But, but, I was supposed to leave with him. I was only supposed to be here two weeks." My cheeks burned with anger. "Why did you send me to clean the bathrooms? I was supposed to leave with him."

Doña Elvira laughed and took the second poblano off the flame. "Who told you that nonsense? You're here to work. You'll stay until the señora throws you out." She handed me the broom. "Consider yourself lucky to have work."

I touched the collar of my uniform and thought of my blue blouse. The one that made me feel like the sky. My grandmother told me that a long time ago the sky had fallen and that that's why we needed to care for the World Tree—to keep the sky in place. I understood why now, because that's the way I felt. Like part of me had caved in.

After that the days dragged by slowly. The next time my father came, I would go home with him. I would not go upstairs to clean the bathrooms. I would run out the door and into his arms and go home to my village and never leave again. Even if the rains never came and the mountain turned into a desert.

One morning there was blood on my sheets when I got out of bed. I gasped when I saw it. I called Doña Elvira. "I think I'm dying," I said. "The gods have come for me during the night, just like they came for my grandmother."

She laughed. "You're not dying, you're just becoming a woman. Didn't your mother prepare you?"

I shook my head. "No."

Doña Elvira rested her hands on her hips. "She didn't tell you anything about becoming a woman?"

I pulled the bedcovers up over the offending stain. "She said there were some things she was going to explain to me when it was time." I looked up. "Is this what she meant?"

Doña Elvira went into her room and came back with some rags. "Here, use these. And go wash your sheets."

I smiled. "I'm a real woman? My mother will be so surprised!"

While we were eating breakfast I pressed Doña Elvira for details. "How long will I be a woman?"

She laughed. "A couple of days every month. You'll get used to it."

"Her Moon time. That's what she called it." I looked at Doña Elvira. "I just didn't understand what she meant."

She reached in the basket for a tortilla. "When my daughter—." Suddenly she broke off in mid-sentence. Her eyes clouded over and she turned them to her plate, where she shoved a spoonful of beans from one side to the other.

"You have a daughter?" I began. "Where is she?"

"Nothing," she said. "Forget it." The anger in her voice returned.

We ate the rest of the meal in silence. After breakfast I went upstairs to clean the bathrooms and we did not speak until much later in the day.

"If you get your work done early I will take you to Mass with me on Sunday," Doña Elvira said that evening. "It will be a special day. We'll celebrate your becoming a woman."

I nodded. "That would be nice, thank you." The patrones went to Mass on Sunday and then out to eat and Doña Elvira had the day off.

She left just after Mass, so I spent most of Sunday alone in the house until late in the afternoon when she came back to make them coffee and a little supper. At first I was lonely, all by myself. But then Sundays became almost a relief. No arguments, no demands, nobody telling me that everything I did wasn't good enough. I could breathe on Sundays.

That Sunday morning I got up extra early and bathed and washed my hair. Doña Elvira helped me with my braids, but she refused to braid in the ribbons the way my mother always did.

"Those ribbons tell everybody you are a village girl. You are a city girl now. You don't need them."

I looked at my reflection in the mirror. "It's our tradition."

She yanked on my hair. "Those aren't traditions. They're stupid superstitions."

"No!" I whirled around and faced her. "No, you don't understand. The way we braid the ribbons in our hair is how we weave the sun into our days."

She snorted. "As if the sun needed you to shine." She turned me back around and continued to braid. "If you're going to be this much trouble, I'll go to Mass without you."

"Our braids are a prayer."

She acted as if she hadn't heard a word. "I don't know why you want that long hair anyway," she said. "You should cut it off. Then you would look like a city girl." She twisted rubber bands on the ends and let them fall against my back.

I looked at her reflection and shook my head. " Our braids are who we are. I will never cut them. If I have to choose, I would rather belong to the sun and my people than to be a city girl."

She smirked. "That nonsense is all right to spout when you're in the village. But you're in the city now and your gods don't live here. You'd better get used to it."

Perhaps she was right. The gods hadn't helped us at all, even in the village. And they had stolen my grandmother and they had dried up our fields and they had made my parents argue and worry all the time. Worse, they had abandoned us. I owed them nothing. I looked at the ribbons, folded them and put them away in the armoire.

We walked along the sidewalk to her church. It was bigger than the one in our village and the priest wore beautiful robes. The altar was covered in an entire mountain of gold and the air was filled with sweet-smelling incense and music that must have come straight from heaven itself. Truly I had found the house of the saints.

We went inside and knelt on a bench. I looked around. "Is this all the saints there are?" I whispered.

She looked up from her prayers. "How many saints do you need, girl?"

I leaned over to her. "These saints have no mirrors. How do you reach their heart?"

She brushed me aside. "Leave me alone, girl. You talk nonsense."

But it wasn't nonsense. It was the way things worked. I got up and knelt in front of a woman saint. Since I had just recently become a woman, I thought she would understand. "Lady Saint," I began. "My breasts are beginning to swell and the patrón stares at me. Sometimes he touches me. He scares me. I don't want to be here any longer. Please send my father to come get me."

I didn't know if she had heard me or not. Without mirrors, it was hard to tell. I couldn't feel her heart and maybe she couldn't feel mine. If Micaela were already a saint she would have understood. She would have sent my father to me. Maybe city saints only understood Spanish. I hoped not.

"Come on, hurry up!" Doña Elvira grabbed me by the arm and pulled me through the heavy door out into the sunlight. "Don't think your prayers will make any difference, because they won't. I prayed for my daughter and she—." Doña Elvira stopped short. The sharp edge returned to her voice. "You're such a dawdler! Come on. It's my day off and I'm not going to waste it taking care of you!"

When we got back to the house Doña Elvira picked up the break-fast dishes and left them by the sink. "I'll be back this afternoon, girl," she said on her way out. "Make sure you have cleaned the kitchen and the bathrooms." She hesitated and her voice softened. "Maybe I'll bring us something special from my village."

I nodded. I had spent three Sundays here already. This Saturday when my father came to collect the money I would go home with him. And I wouldn't come back.

Chapter Four

"Rosa!"

His voice startled me. I dropped the little doll I was making out of scraps of material and looked up to see the patrón standing in the doorway to the kitchen. I didn't know there was anyone in the house.

"Rosa, what are you doing?" He towered over me, eyes bulging with red veins.

I glanced up at him briefly, and then lowered my eyes. My heart pounded and my lip trembled. "Nothing, señor. Do you need something?" I stood up and smoothed the dress over my legs. The way he looked at me, I felt naked.

He studied me, his eyes traveling up and down my body, touching with his gaze, touching with his voice, touching with his presence. I held the doll between us and wished with all my heart for Saint John the Baptist.

"Do you know how to prepare coffee?"

The veins on his neck stood out, purple against the red of his face. I had seen Doña Elvira prepare coffee. It seemed easy enough. I nodded. "Yes, señor."

He turned and stomped out of the room. "Then prepare me one." The kitchen door swung behind him.

I let out my breath and lay my doll on the counter. I filled the coffee pot with water and put it on the stove to boil. Then I opened the bag of coffee and poured the beans out. My hands were shaking. I wanted to do it just right so that he would not be angry. I wanted to show him respect. How much did Doña Elvira use? I had never noticed. I took a deep breath and I promised myself and all the gods I would pay more attention next time.

"Rosa!"

I let out a stifled cry and whirled around.

The patrón was standing right behind me. His breath, hot and damp against my face, smelled of garlic and stale cigarettes. "Take off your uniform."

I looked into his eyes and clutched at the collar of my dress. Beads of sweat glistened on his face. I shook my head. "Excuse me, señor?"

He stepped toward me and I backed into the counter. My legs shook, my knees buckled, my whole body trembled. What did he want? I leaned back across the counter as far away from him as I could.

He grabbed my hand and pulled it away. "Take off your uniform!"

He frightened me and I screamed. He clamped his hand across my mouth. He ripped open my uniform and grabbed me by the neck. "Into your room. Now!" In my room he threw me onto the cot. Then he was on top of me, reaching between my legs, grunting, panting, sweating. I didn't understand what he was doing, what he wanted. And then I felt him. I cried out. He slapped me. "Shut up!"

He pushed and grunted, pushed and sweated and stank. Pushed and didn't care that I cried. A wild animal raged inside of him, unleashing its cruelty in the worst way. The weight of his body bore down, secreted its smell, secreted its sweat, secreted its angry essence into mine. After a long time he stopped, stood up, and closed his pants. "If you tell anyone about this, it will go badly for you."

I didn't move.

He left my room. "You'd better come take this pot off the fire," he called. "All the water is gone."

I stood up, staggered into the kitchen and took the empty pot off the fire. Then I went back to my room and fell onto the bed. It was the last place I wanted to be, the place that held his smell, but there was nowhere else. I felt sick. My arms hurt where he had held me; my head was spinning and blood trickled out from between my legs.

The light in the sky had turned orange. I sat up on the edge of my bed and tried to close my uniform, but the buttons lay scattered about the floor. I reached to pick them up but vomited instead. Then the orange gave way to darkness and a chill settled over the room. It was dark when I regained my senses.

I dragged myself into the shower. What had happened? I couldn't make any sense of it. His smell was everywhere. In my face, in my nose, in my hair. I couldn't breathe, his smell suffocated me. I shuddered. He was all over me again. With me still. Panting and pushing and sweating. Waves of fear and repulsion rose from my gut. I threw up again. I collapsed onto the floor and cried. He had hurt me. He knew and didn't care. And I had been powerless to stop him.

The grief in me sobbed until my insides hurt and no more tears came. I put on a clean uniform. Soon everyone would be back. I went into the kitchen and knelt on the kitchen floor to pick up the buttons. Scattered white buttons. I used to pick white flowers for the Virgin. White was her favorite color, next to blue. I clutched the buttons in my hand. Couldn't they be flower petals instead? Just for one moment, couldn't I go back home and give her the flowers I had picked? Couldn't I? I opened my hand. My flower petals had become buttons. I felt sick. My grandmother had been right. I had prayed the wrong prayer.

I left the buttons on a shelf in the armoire and turned to my cot, pulled the sheets off and stumbled up the spiral staircase to the washboard on the roof. The next thing I knew the sky was turning dark and Doña Elvira was looking over my shoulder.

"Why are you washing your sheets at this time of night, girl?"

I jumped.

Doña Elvira stood behind me, her hands on her hips. "Don't you have any brains at all? Tonight you will sleep on your bare mattress." She stepped closer to the washboard and inspected the sheets. "What, your period again? How often are you going to bleed?"

I choked when I tried to answer.

She turned away and went down the stairs to the kitchen and I bent over the washboard and scrubbed harder. Scrubbed and scrubbed until my knuckles bled. Cried and scrubbed and bled. And the wet sheet was full of him, of me and of pain.

From below Doña Elvira's voice ripped through the night air. "Rosa, are you going to stay up there all night?"

I cleared my throat and wiped my eyes with my apron. "Do you need something?"

"I've made us some hot chocolate. I brought it from my village."

"All right." I wrung out the sheets, trying to squeeze the memory of what had happened out of my mind, demanding, begging, pleading that it not be true.

She looked across the table at me. "Have you been crying?"

I turned my face to the window.

In the reflection of the glass I saw the kitchen door swing open. The patrón went to the bottle of drinking water and poured himself a glass. He turned to us and spoke, holding the glass across his chest. "Doña Elvira, you must teach this girl to make coffee. Today I asked her for a coffee and she nearly burned the pot."

He turned away, tilted the glass up to his mouth and emptied it. Then he turned back. "I'll be working at home on Sunday afternoons for a while and I'll expect her to take care of me." He set the empty glass down on the counter with a thud and walked out of the kitchen. "Make sure she does." The door swung behind him.

I grasped my shoulders, lowered my chin onto my chest and closed my eyes. Please, Saint John the Baptist, I have to get out of here. I have to get back home. The saints here only speak Spanish and have no mirrors. Please help me. I'm going to die in this place if you don't.

"Yes, señor." Doña Elvira nodded at the swinging door and then looked at me for a long time. Then she sighed a deep sigh, as if her body had suddenly become too heavy for its frame. She lowered her eyes, picked up the cup of hot chocolate with both hands, held it to her lips for a moment as if making a decision, and then drank.

Chapter Five

Doña Elvira wondered why I hung my towel over the mirror on the armoire that night. "It'll never get dry. Put it upstairs on the line with your sheets."

I pretended I hadn't heard her. I couldn't bear to look at myself or the place where it had happened. That night I lay down on the floor, but she came into my room and dragged me up by the arm.

"You'll sleep in the bed! You're not in your village anymore!" Her words burned in my head.

The next morning I broke a vase. It was the vase the señora's flowers had been in. It slipped out of my fingers and onto the floor.

Doña Elvira was at my side in an instant. "Stupid girl, why are you so clumsy today? Can't you do anything right? We'll both get into trouble if the patrona finds out." She brought some newspaper to wrap the broken glass in. "Here, wrap it in this first. Did you cut yourself?"

I shook my head.

"Then don't cry." She put the bundled glass in a plastic bag and tied it shut. "Quit feeling sorry for yourself. It doesn't get you anywhere." She opened the trashcan and buried the bundle deep inside. "Now pay attention to what you're doing. You'll get us both fired. You don't want to be out on the street!"

I wiped my cheeks and stared into the soapy water in front of me. I wanted to tell her what he had done to me. I wanted to tell her that no matter how angry the señora might be over the vase, it didn't scare me nearly as much as the thought of him. Nothing could match the terror I felt.

I didn't know if she would she believe me or say it was my fault. If she would scold me or protect me. Or if she would tell my father. What would he say? That I had let him down? That I had betrayed his trust? I remembered the last day of my grandmother's life, when I lied to her. That's what this was. It was my punishment. I had brought shame on us. It would have to be my secret.

I finished the dishes and went upstairs to clean the bathrooms. His scent consumed the air—in the shower, in the bedroom, in the dirty clothes. I gagged, tried not to vomit. His scent forced itself into my nose, into my throat, into my lungs, left me gasping for air and clawing for escape. I leaned against the window and forced it open, breathed in clean air, air that had none of him in it. I threw some water on the floor, mopped the bathroom and got out as quickly as I could.

I took my bucket into the señora's bathroom. It smelled of perfume. Too much perfume, the same way she did. Doña Elvira's voice called from below.

"Girl, hurry up. I need to get to the market."

I turned back to the bathroom, knelt down and began scrubbing the floor. I folded myself up into a tiny bundle and scrubbed the floor, wishing it were my body. I tried to scrub out everything that had happened. I wanted to scrub out the past weeks, this house, this city, my life.

"Girl!" Doña Elvira's voice rang shrilly in my ear. "Why do you scrub the same spot over and over when there is the whole bathroom to clean? Have you not learned anything?"

Her feet were planted in front of my scrub brush. I didn't need to look up to know that her hands were on her hips and her face bore an angry look. Anger and sadness—that's all there was in this house.

I moved the brush to a different spot and continued scrubbing tiny circles—tiny, tiny circles. My grandmother said the circle was sacred. She said it represented the god of the sun and of the eternity of life. These circles were not sacred. These circles went nowhere and stood for nothing.

That Wednesday I hurried to finish the bathrooms and left the house before the patrones came home for lunch. I closed the door behind me and stood for a moment on the spot where I had last been with my father. What had I said to him? I had told him he would be proud of me. I took a deep breath and my eyes filled with tears again. My voice wavered, but I said the words anyway, pretending he could hear. "Oh, Papí, I'm so sorry. I have brought a terrible shame on the family. Please forgive me."

I wiped my tears on the back of my hand and walked to the corner. My magic shoes hadn't kept me safe after all. Maybe they didn't have real magic. Maybe it was just city magic they had. The tiny bits of color inside sparkled as before, but I couldn't hear any giggles, just the dull plop-plop of my feet against the pavement stones. I looked at the street sign again and sounded out the letters. "Al-cah-lah." How could it still be the same name when everything else in the world had changed? Grandmother had said that everything a person does affects every other person and that was why we had to be mindful of our actions. Perhaps those rules only applied to the center of the universe. Maybe that's what the saints knew and that's why they didn't bother to answer prayers in the city.

A loud noise startled me. I looked up in time to see the smoke from a rocket in the sky. It must be a festival. Boom! Another rocket. I stepped off the curb and walked in the direction of the noise. The festivals in my village were the best times of the year. Dances and horse races and sweets and fireworks. Perhaps the saints were here. The real saints. The ones with mirrors.

In my village I liked the festival of Saint John the Baptist best. We wore our nicest clothes and for weeks beforehand my mother would mend and wash them. Sometimes she would sew on new ribbons. Maybe Saint John the Baptist had come to this festival. Maybe he had heard my prayer. I crossed the street toward the celebration.

A band played. I followed the sound through the streets and around a corner to a little square. Lots of people had come out of their shops to watch. There was a puppet show and a man who swallowed fire. He poured gasoline on a rag tied to the end of a stick and lit it and put it in my mouth. I was glad I didn't have to do that. Maybe Doña Elvira was right. Maybe you had to do things like that out on the street. A man with a music machine had a monkey dressed in a red suit. The man played a tune and the monkey walked around and asked people to put money in its hat. I turned away. The monkey reminded me of him. I shuddered.

My father had always taken me to the festivals. His grip was strong and sure and when I was with him I felt that everything was right and perfect. I wished he were here now. I imagined my father walking with me, hearing his voice, holding his hand in mine, and tasting all the things I was seeing for the first time – like the little cups of the fruits called nances and baskets piled high with sweet breads decorated with pink and green and colored tops.

"Are you thirsty?"

I turned around. A boy about my age was standing just behind me. His eyes were kind.

I blushed. "A little."

He reached into the pocket of his pants and pulled out a coin. "I have enough to buy us each a drink, if you want." He wore dark blue pants that were torn and dirty and too big for him. A rope belt tied around his waist held them up. Concrete dust covered his pants, his arms and his hair. A shirt that had once been white, now tattered and gray, was partly tucked in his pants.

I nodded. "Okay." I remembered how parched my mouth used to get in the heat of the festivals in those spring afternoons. Dust filled every space, including my mouth, until I could barely talk. Paciencia, my father would say with a wink. And sure enough the first mouthful of our cold mountain water always made me forget my earlier thirst and sent shivers throughout my body.

The boy gave the drink vendor the coin and pointed to a bottle of colored water. The vendor poured equal amounts into two small plastic bags, stood a straw in them, tied them with a rubber band and gave them to the boy.

The boy had a big smile on his face when he gave me one. "Here you are."

I blushed. "Thank you." I took the drink from his outstretched hand and put my mouth to the straw. Not shockingly cold like our mountain water, the drink was pleasantly sweet and comforting. "It's good," I said.

He didn't say anything.

For a while we stood on the curb and watched the puppet show. "I like the fireworks best."

He took a sip of his drink. "Me too. I like the way the gunpowder smells." He grinned. "Peppery."

I looked at him. "It is, isn't it? I had never thought of it like that."

He smiled and looked down. "Those shoes." He looked up at me. "They look like they have fireworks inside them."

I laughed. "Fireworks?"

He grinned. "Yeah, fireworks. They do."

I turned away. "You're crazy. Whoever heard of fireworks in shoes?"

"They would take you lots of places in a hurry."

"Oh, but they do. They have magic inside them." I waited a moment. "Do you know about magic?"

He shrugged. "I know that magic in the city doesn't always work." A grin slid across his face. "But then again, sometimes it does—like today."

My hands flew up to cover my embarrassment. It was too much. This boy, the festival, the music—more wonderful than I could take in. I knew I wanted this boy to be my friend. I wanted to talk with him and laugh and tell funny stories the way Micaela and I had always done. I had a feeling if I could do that, everything would be okay.

After the puppet show was over he said he had to go back to work. His eyes sparkled when he told me. "I have a job. I work in a hardware store." He grinned and took the last sip of his drink.

I did the same.

"I'm going to earn a lot of money and save it. When I go back to my village I will have enough to build a house with two rooms and a roof."

"I think you will, too. And it will be a pretty house, I'm sure of it." I thought about my house, the one my father had built. "My house has two rooms."

He smiled. "Yes, it's the way to build a house. That's the way I'm going to build mine."

I had never thought about how many rooms a house could or should have. I had never seen a house with more than two rooms—before I came to the city. "Well, good luck. And thanks for the drink."

He smiled and disappeared into the crowd. When I couldn't see him anymore, I looked down at my shoes. They did look like they had fireworks inside. I decided that every time I looked at them, I would remember him. The thought made me happy.

I stayed a while longer remembering the good times at the festivals in our village. Like the time I ate three elotes and my mother was afraid I would be sick from so much corn. Or when my father took me to the chapel where the autoridades met with the gods. When my grandmother called the gods and the way the candles would flicker, one at a time, as each god arrived. The way the night sky lit up with brilliant colors and loud popping noises.

The happy feelings of the festival stayed with me until I reached the corner of Alcalá, the street that didn't notice that my life had changed. In my village every person and every tree would have noticed. How could they not? We were all threads woven on the same loom. I didn't want to go back into that house. I didn't want to belong to those people—too much sadness, too much anger and too much perfume. Instead I walked around the block. Once, then again, then more times than I could count.

On Saturday my father came. I heard the bell. I knew it had to be him. He always came right after breakfast. This time Doña Elvira said I should go outside and talk to him, but instead I grabbed my bucket and hurried past her up the stairs.

Doña Elvira stood at the foot of the stairs. "Don't you want to see your father?"

"I don't have time right now. The guests will be arriving soon. I have too much to do." I called. How could I face him now? He would know.

"Girl, you need to see your father."

I shook my head. Could I risk looking into his eyes and seeing the disgust that had to be there? There was enough pain in my life already. Instead I scrubbed tiny circles in the bathroom.

Doña Elvira came up the staircase calling me. "Girl!"

"Tell him I'm busy but I'll see him next time he comes for sure."

Doña Elvira came into the señora's bedroom where the señora sat at her dressing table, putting on makeup. "This new girl certainly does a good job on the bathrooms," she said. She spoke about me as if I weren't in the doorway of the next room.

Doña Elvira shrugged. "She's just a child. I think she likes to play in the water."

She traced her fingers across her cheek. "Yes, she's young, isn't she?" She looked at herself in the mirror and patted her face with powder. "Is her father still downstairs?"

"Yes."

"What does he want?"

Doña Elvira turned to me. "He wants to see her. Make sure she's okay."

The señora leaned back from her dressing table and looked at me. "Are you?"

Tears filled my eyes. "Yes, señora."

She stared at me for a moment, then she turned to Doña Elvira. "Tell him she's fine and that she'll go home this Wednesday." She reached into her purse, took out some money and handed it to Doña Elvira. "Give him her pay."

Doña Elvira nodded. "Yes, señora."

The señora reached for a pair of earrings. "And then make sure he leaves."

That Sunday I went to Mass with Doña Elvira, and knelt in front of the lady saint.

"Do you remember me? I came to talk to you last week. I'm Rosa."

I waited, but her face didn't change. She stared ahead as if she didn't even notice I was there. I looked around. There had to be a saint with a mirror. At least one. Without mirrors there was no way to reach them.

"Please tell me how to reach your heart. In my village all the saints wear mirrors on their chests, so that we can sit in their heart when we talk to them. But here in the city things are different. Can you tell me how to talk to your heart?"

Again I waited, but there was no reaction from the lady saint. "Well, goodbye, then." I got up and looked at the other people who were praying. They lit candles, they knelt, they prayed, but their faces didn't change for them either. Suddenly I understood. I got up and waited for Doña Elvira by the door. There was no sense praying to a saint that had no heart.

Sunday afternoon after everybody had left and the house was empty, I climbed up on the roof and squeezed myself in behind the water tank.

"Rosa!"

My stomach tightened into a knot when the patrón called my name. I didn't answer.

"Rosa!" His voice strained. I saw his face everywhere. The veins stood out on his neck, thick and purple. His eyes bulged. "Where are you?" From the sound of his voice I knew he stood at the foot of the spiral staircase. His words unleashed a fury like that of vicious dogs. They tore angrily through the metal staircase and rampaged across the rooftop, slashing and tearing everything they found. I was terrified, even of them.

My stomach clenched tighter and I crouched in the space between the wall and the water tank. Please, Saint John the Baptist, please don't let him find me.

"Rosa, come here at once. I order you!"

I buried my face in my hands so he wouldn't hear me sobbing. His voice was hoarse and sounded desperate. The sound of my own breathing frightened me. Could he hear it? I listened for footsteps on the metal staircase, but all I heard was the pounding of the hollow drum in my chest. I clasped my hands over my ears and tried to drown out all the sounds. When the day began to fade and the birds stopped chattering, I heard voices and the clatter of dishes below in the kitchen.

Doña Elvira was angry. "Where were you all afternoon, girl?"

I looked down at the floor. "I was hanging up the wash," I stammered.

"All afternoon?"

I shrugged. "I forgot about the time."

Doña Elvira's face was flushed. "Haven't you learned anything? Don't you know what your responsibilities are?" She stared at the orange and blue tiles on the wall. "It's nothing what you have to do here, do you understand? It's much worse out on the street."

She stopped, doubled her hands into fists and pounded on the counter. "If you disappear again I will beat you and send you back to your father."

I hung my head. A beating would be all right, welcome even. I deserved that and worse. But I could not go back to my father, much as I wanted to. Not anymore.

Chapter Six

The next Sunday the patrón ordered me to prepare coffee again. My hand shook as I filled the pot with water and I struggled not to spill it on the low flame. He grabbed my neck, shoved me into my room, and threw me onto the narrow bed. I tried to find a place to hide, to get away, a dead place inside of me where he couldn't reach me. Lying on the cot I tried not to feel the drops of his sweat on my face, tried not to feel his suffocating bulk, tried not to hear the grunting and panting in my ear, tried not to smell the cigarettes and garlic that issued from his mouth, tried not to cry as he hurt me.

When he finished there was still a little water left in the pot. "Do you want coffee now?" I asked.

He looked at me with disgust. "Not from your hands, you dirty Indian." He walked out of the kitchen and I turned off the flame.

In the shower I crouched on the floor and let the water run over me, but I couldn't get away from it. The black, nameless, formless it that began to suffocate me, color me, control me, decide who I was, determine my fate, choose my thoughts, direct my actions. It began to take over my life and slowly squeeze me out. A long while later I pulled myself out of the shower and put on my uniform. Then I took my sheets up to the rooftop. The scabs on my knuckles opened again on the washboard, but the pain felt almost welcome. Blood and pain and water and him—they mingled again as if each were a part of the other.

"Why do you persist in washing your sheets so late in the day?"

51

Doña Elvira demanded.

I didn't look up from the washboard; I just shook my head. "I didn't have time before." I didn't want her to see my face. Not even her.

She put her things down and came closer, inspecting my work. "You'll wear them out, washing them every week. And look at you—there's another button off your uniform—you are such a careless child!"

I didn't answer. I kept on scrubbing. When my knuckles were numb and my hands were too cold to feel anything, I wrung out the sheets. I wanted to wring out my body. To rid it of the unholy alliance that had moved in.

The days began to turn cooler. One day the señora came in with an armload of marigolds. "Tomorrow is el Día de los Muertos," she announced. "You haven't forgotten?"

I blushed. I almost had forgotten. "No, señora." I had been looking forward to the Day of the Dead for the entire month, thinking I would be home. Instead I was here. "Will you be going to the cemetery?" I asked.

The señora looked at me uncomprehendingly "Of course. Why wouldn't we?"

Suddenly I was embarrassed. Of course they would. They had family. I was the only one who would be alone.

She brushed past me with the flowers and laid them in the sink. "Take care of these for me until tomorrow." The kitchen door swung behind her. "Make sure they stay fresh."

"Yes, señora."

When the kitchen door stopped swinging I took a single marigold. Then I reached under the cabinet, pulled out an empty soda bottle, filled it with water and put the flower in it. Just like I had done at home. Except here white flowers for the Virgin had become yellow flowers for the dead.

I went to my room, set the soda bottle on the shelf of the armoire and shut the door. The next day, as soon as the patrones had left, I pulled out the candle I had brought from home and lit it. A bit of melted wax on the shelf held it firm. Just like my grandmother and I had done.

I watched the candle flame and thought of my grandmother, willing her to come. I had nothing of hers to entice her with, nor did I have any special foods to treat her spirit after the long journey, but I hoped she'd be able to find me anyway.

All of a sudden the door flew open and Doña Elvira burst into my room. "What are you doing, girl?" she shrieked. "Trying to set the house on fire?"

I looked up. "It's just a candle for Muertos."

She stepped across the room and yanked the candle out of the armoire.

"I was waiting for my grandmother to come," I said.

Doña Elvira shook her head. "You nearly burned the entire armoire, do you know that?" She pointed to the dark spot above the shelf. "How are you going to explain that to the señora?"

I shrugged. "I'm sorry." But really I wasn't. I didn't care if it burned down or not. I would have been happy if the whole house had burned. I would have cheered.

Doña Elvira thrust the candle into my hands. "Blow it out. Your grandmother's not coming."

I blew out my candle. A wisp of smoke made an attempt to reform itself in the air, but then slowly dissolved and I knew that, for the first time in my life, I was truly alone.

Later that evening Doña Elvira called me into the kitchen. "Come and sit down. Let's have some hot chocolate. I'll make it with milk instead of water tonight. "

I slumped down into the chair at the little red table. "Have you been to the cemetery already?"

She nodded. "Of course. I went this past weekend."

Of course. She had gone home to her village and had made her trip to the cemetery while she was there. I wish I could go home. Better not to even think it anymore.

"I bought some thread at the market," she said, bending over the stove and lowering the flame.

I thought of the flowers my mother and I had embroidered. When I still had silly childish dreams. I forced myself to speak. "Yes? What colors?"

"I'll show you." She left the stove and strode into her room. A moment later she returned, carrying a small plastic bag.

"I thought you might like to make a little gift to send to your mother —something pretty." She pulled out a round wooden hoop and two pieces of material imprinted with a design, which she laid on the table between us. "I have red, and blue, and yellow…" She named each color as she pulled out the spools, one by one. "Brown, and two shades of green, a pink, and an orange." She looked up at me. "These will make a pretty bouquet, won't they? "

I nodded.

She took her place opposite me. "Your mother taught you how to embroider, didn't she?"

My face burned at the memory of the flowers I had embroidered, thinking my father and I would sell them in the city. It burned at the realization of my own foolishness. Of my silly dreams. I remembered that day on the bus, how my father wouldn't look at me, how he didn't laugh, and how he had walked away from me in front of the señora's house. Now I understood. It was always the plan, I just didn't know it. He never intended to sell my flowers, just me.

Doña Elvira pulled out two needles and handed me one. "Here, why don't we begin now? The light is still good."

I took the needle and stared at the threads, unable to make a decision. My father had abandoned me. Finally she put one of the cloths in my hands and handed me a spool of thread. "Why don't you start with pink? It's a good color for roses."

Hot tears erupted from my eyes and rolled down my cheeks as I threaded the needle. My father had known exactly what he was doing.

Her voice was stern. "Girl, we have to take what comes along for us in this life. Nobody's going to rescue you. Not your father, not the saints. You just have to take it."

I looked up at her. "You could help me."

She shook her head. "I don't meddle. At my age, I can't afford to be out on the street."

"Please."

She picked up a needle and unwound a length of brown thread, broke it, then twisted it into a knot. "It's none of my business what goes on."

I felt his hand grab my throat and the stench of his breath in my nostrils. I put the embroidery down, lay the needle across the top with pink thread still in it, and ran up the circular staircase to the roof.

She ran after me, reaching out to stop me on the top step. "Don't you think your father knew what was going to happen?"

I backed away. It wasn't true. She didn't know my father. I inched away, seeking refuge in the darkness of the rooftop. "What do you mean?"

She matched my steps, following me onto the roof, her face nearly in mine. "You're not the first girl from your village to come to the city, are you?"

I backed away. "No."

She put her hands on her hips, the way she did when she wanted to be right. "And where are they—the others?"

I shook my head and backed away. "I don't know. They were older. I never paid that much attention." I turned my back on her. I didn't want to hear any more.

She continued. "And you never heard talk about them?"

I shook my head. "No."

"When you go home, look around. Most of them never went back."

I ran to the edge of the rooftop. "You don't know you're saying. You don't know me or my family or my village. You're just a mean old woman," I sobbed. "I don't know what are you talking about!"

Her voice sliced the night air like a knife. "You know what I'm talking about. The city is full of men like the patrón. Men who have their way with young Indian girls. Your father knew that when he brought you here."

I whirled around, my hand raised to slap her face. "No! It's not true! My father would never hurt me. He loves me."

She grabbed my hand and glared, forcing her truth into my mind. "Your father sold you, girl."

"No!" I screamed. "You lie!" But I knew she spoke the truth.

I came to dread Sundays. I dreaded the screaming silence of the house, then the click of the key in the front door, the squeak of shoes against the tile floor. I dreaded the swish of the kitchen door, the wheezing breath, the grunting in my ear, the squeak of the rusty metal bed frame hitting against the wall. Then, at last, the sound of his zipper and the slam of the door. Another Sunday was over and I had survived.

One Wednesday I went to the church and knelt before Saint Michael. I looked up at him. "I spit into the patron's coffee today," I said. "I'm not sorry. I'm just telling you. You can punish me if you like. But I'd do it again." I looked around. People whispered prayers and lit candles. Nobody talked. I looked back at Saint Michael. "He says I'm bad." I looked at the snake at Saint Michael's feet and then up at his face. "Am I?"

Saint Michael stared past me as if he hadn't heard.

I left the church and walked the streets. Doña Elvira said it was better to be dead than on the street. How much worse could it be?

I saw a woman walking toward me on the sidewalk. She was a señora, a householder. She would be able to help me. I could tell her what had happened. She would understand and take me with her, protect me. I smiled hopefully. She smiled back. When she got close I stopped her. "Please, señora, I beg you, help me."

Her smile quickly became disgust. She pulled away, brushed the sleeve I had touched, clutched her purse to her chest and hurried off. I stood there for a moment remembering Doña Elvira's admonition. Nobody was going to help me. I turned walked slowly back to the house. Where else was there to go?

At the house I tried to help Doña Elvira so she wouldn't be angry. There were already too many angry people in one house. One Saturday Doña Elvira was very busy. "I'll vacuum the living room for you," I volunteered.

"Do you know how?"

I nodded. I had seen her push it back and forth and I had heard the noise it made. It seemed easy.

"Good, then I can go to the meat market." She left the house with her market bag and I took out the vacuum and placed it in the middle of the room and pushed, but it didn't make the noise. I pushed harder, but nothing happened and the rug was just as dirty as before.

There was no one at home. I sat down on the sofa and put my feet up and pretended I was the señora. What fun to have such a big house and so many pretty things. I scanned the room. Maybe I would take something. Steal it. Maybe I would. I'd take it and sell it in the market and buy myself something pretty. In all the time I'd worked there, I'd never had a cent of my own. The señora had given my father all of my money. Come Wednesday, I'd take something and not feel at all sorry about it.

A key turned. I jumped up. The door opened and Doña Elvira walked through carrying a papaya under her arm. Her market bag bulged in the other hand. She glanced at the rug. "Did you vacuum?"

I shook my head. "It's not working. I'll get the broom."

She handed me the market bag and took the papaya into the kitchen. Then she motioned for me to follow her back into the living room. "Show me what you did."

I rolled the vacuum back and forth.

She started laughing. "Ay, niña! You have to plug it in!"

I blushed and covered my face with my hands.

As the winter progressed, I hid more often in the dead place I had constructed inside of me. I retreated more and more often into that place until finally I could no longer hear my grandmother's stories in my head, couldn't remember how my father's hand felt, didn't remember Micaela's laughter or the way my mother's arms used to cradle me. I began to forget who I was, who they were, and who we together were. Sometimes it seemed as though this wasn't happening to me at all—it felt like I was watching somebody else.

Spring arrived before things started to get better. One Wednesday I went into the church and knelt before one of the lady saints. "I thought you weren't listening to me, but I was wrong. My problems from being a woman are going away. I don't bleed anymore." I took a deep breath. "So thank you." I turned to leave, then turned back. "The only problem is some things are making me sick. Like Sundays. And coffee."

On the way out I lit a candle for my grandmother and ran my fingers along the belt that she and I had made. I wanted to pull her words out and wrap them around me, but I couldn't hear them.

That Sunday the patrón grabbed me by the arm and pulled me into my room. His body exuded sweat and the stench of stale cigarettes.

"Now you know how it feels to be used," he whispered hoarsely.

I turned my face toward the wall and reached for the dead place.

"In this life everybody uses everybody else. Nobody cares about anybody in this world." His voice was urgent, as though he were anxious to be rid of the terrible truth he had discovered. "Do you know how that feels? To know that nobody cares about you?"

I did.

I felt his body tense and then the weight of his sorrow collapsed on me. A moment later he stood up and closed his pants. "You count for nothing, do you understand? Nothing. You are disposable."

He was right. My own family had thrown me out.

When he left, I got up and went into the kitchen, opened the drawer and took out a knife. I lifted it to one side of my head and cut off a braid. It fell to the floor. Then I cut the other one. For a while I stared at them, lying askew on the floor. They didn't belong to me. I no longer had the right to wear them. Braids were for people who lived with honor and family and love and tradition. It no longer mattered that the sun went into the Underworld each night and rose victorious again each morning. I wasn't a child of the sun anymore. It was like the patrón said: I was disposable. I picked the braids up off the floor, tossed them into the trashcan and closed the lid.

Chapter Seven

On Wednesday I saw the boy from the festival again. I wanted to run to him and tell him everything and at the same time I wanted to run away so he wouldn't see what I had become. I turned my face away and pretended I hadn't seen him, but he crossed the street and stopped in front of me.

"Hi."

I looked down at the pavement. "Hi."

"Are you still working?"

I nodded without looking up.

"You cut your hair."

I turned away. He saw too much.

"It looks good. You have beautiful hair. Is this your afternoon off?"

"Yes."

"I have some free time. Would you like to walk for a while?"

I shook my head. "No, I can't."

"I've been looking for you ever since that day at the festival."

I looked up at him. "You have?"

He nodded and scuffed his shoe against the pavement. "I thought we could be friends."

I lowered my gaze. "That would be nice. I don't have any friends in the city."

"So will you walk with me to my work?"

I shook my head. Why didn't he say anything? He had noticed my hair right away. He had to notice my belly. What was I going to say?

He shrugged. "Well, okay then. Maybe I'll see you again sometime."

"Maybe."

He walked away, then stopped and turned back to me. "It was never your hair anyway. It was your eyes. They carry the light of the sun."

I watched as he walked away and turned the corner, wishing I were walking with him, guessing I could tell him everything, knowing he would understand. Instead, I had let him go, and now it was just me, alone, ashamed and afraid.

"Now we know what you have been doing on your afternoons off!" The patrona grabbed me by the shoulders and shook me; her voice shrieked. "Aren't you ashamed? You people are nothing but animals!" She turned away and strode through the swinging door. Her voice rang in from the dining room. "These Indians, they are all the same. You give them a job and a place to live and food and this is how they repay you. I don't know why we bother."

Doña Elvira glared at me. "Now you're in real trouble. You should have tried to hide it a while longer." She pulled out a stack of stale tortillas and motioned for me to chop an onion.

I shrugged and walked over to the cutting board to one side of the burners.

She reached up for a bottle of oil and poured half of it into the earthenware casserole on the stove. Chilaquiles again. "You'll be lucky if the patrón doesn't throw you out."

I chopped the onion, pulled out the molcajete and began to mash the chili peppers. I winced as they burned my knuckles.

Doña Elvira glanced at me. "No sense in trying so hard. Those sheets will never come clean. They were soiled before you got here."

She cut the stale tortillas into strips and I shredded the cheese. When the patrón came home the señora brought him into the kitchen. She was still upset, but he spoke kindly to me.

"Come here, girl."

I stiffened as his hand gripped the back of my neck.

"Now why have you gotten yourself pregnant? Don't you know any better?" He squeezed my neck and without waiting for an answer he turned to the señora. "You know Indian girls do this sort of thing." In a soothing voice he told the señora this was her chance to be a good Christian. "Your charity will earn you a good place in heaven, my dear."

The señora stared at my belly.

The patrón slid his hand down from my neck to my shoulder, announcing to everyone that he owned me. "She will stay and work for now."

His hand gripped my shoulder tightly. "Her family is counting on the money. When it's time for the baby, she'll have to leave."

He turned to Doña Elvira. "I'm sorry to put you to so much trouble. I know how hard you've worked with this girl." He looked up and down my body, as if touching me one day a week wasn't enough. "Maybe you can bring a girl from your village. A young one, easy to train."

I lowered my eyes and clenched my jaw. A mixture of feelings flooded my body. Loathing. Humiliation. I pressed my lips together to stop myself from blurting out the truth. No one present wanted to hear the truth. They all knew it anyway.

Doña Elvira half-closed her eyes and nodded. "I'll see what I can do."

The patrones went into the dining room and Doña Elvira served lunch. The house was unusually quiet that day, on both sides of the swinging door.

After lunch we cleared the dishes. Doña Elvira usually left them to me to wash, but today she hovered. She wet a dishcloth and wiped the stovetop. "You do understand why your belly is growing, don't you?"

I stared at the soapy water in front of me. I didn't want to talk. "I've been eating too much."

She slapped the dishcloth down beside the sink. "Don't be stupid. You've seen women with big bellies before. You know what it means."

I shook my head. "Yes, but they were having babies." It happened to them, but not to me. I was not going to have a baby. Not by him. Not this way. I reached into the soapy water, pulled out a plate and wiped it with the sponge.

Her face was in mine. "And you think you're not?

I didn't want to hear these words. Why did she keep talking? Did she like making me suffer? "I don't want a baby." I rinsed the plate and set it in the drainer. "I don't want anything from this house."

She stared at me for a moment, then picked up the dishcloth again and mopped a pool of water on the counter. "If you're lucky it will die."

I plunged my hands back into the soapy water. "Maybe I'll be lucky."

"Then when it's over you can go home."

I washed another plate. "No. I'll die with it."

Doña Elvira dropped the dishcloth onto the counter and buried her face in her hands. "No, not that. Not again."

Sunday, Sunday, always Sunday. My hatred of Sunday grew so large, it was all I could see. Every day became the day before or the day after, or three days before or three days after. It didn't matter which way I counted, Sunday dominated every week, even during the time of the posadas. Even Christmas had a Sunday on either side.

"You had to go and get yourself pregnant, you stupid girl," the patrón whispered into my ear as he lay on top of me. "Don't you know how much trouble you have caused me?" His breath was hot and moist and heavy.

I clenched my jaw and stared at the wall behind him. In spite of my hatred for it, my belly continued to grow. As soon as Christmas Day passed the señora insisted I leave. She said I was to wait for my father and to go with him, but he didn't come that Saturday, so she paid me for the week and told me to get out.

Doña Elvira was upset. She took off her apron and threw it on the counter. "They ask too much of me."

I nodded. The guests would be arriving soon and she would spend the entire day and most of the night in the kitchen. "I know. It's Saturday."

She sat down at the little red table and buried her face in her hands. "Do you know how many girls I've had to bring?"

I finished sweeping and put away the broom. "Then don't bring another one."

She wiped her face with the back of her hand. "He'll throw me out if I don't."

I fingered the lock on the patio door. She was afraid to be on the street. Terrible things happened on the street. "You can work someplace else."

She shook her head. "It wouldn't be any different."

I turned my back. "Then tell her not to make coffee on Sunday afternoons."

She got up from the table and hurried out of the kitchen. I went into my room to gather my things. I took off my uniform, pulled my blue blouse over my head, and wrapped my black woolen skirt around my bulging waistline. I fastened it with the belt and stuffed my things into a plastic bag. Before I left I knocked on Doña Elvira's door.

"Who is it?"

I opened the door a crack. "It's me."

She was sitting on the edge of her bed, holding a photograph. She looked up.

I stood in the doorway. "I came to say goodbye."

She stood up and showed me the photograph. It was a girl that looked like me. I looked at the photograph and then at Doña Elvira.

She tilted her head to one side. "You reminded me of her."

I didn't ask, but I could tell from the look on her face that it wasn't good. I nodded and left. No sense in both of us crying.

The señora was waiting in the dining room. She held out her hand. "Give me your bag, girl."

Girl. I wasn't real to her and she wasn't real to me. I handed it to her and watched as she dumped my belongings out. A red hair ribbon, a plastic comb, a picture of the Virgin, the stub of a candle and a bouquet of embroidered flowers on a cloth that a little more than year ago had held my hopes for the future.

She rummaged through my things. "You'd better not be taking anything that doesn't belong to you." She turned away and went into the living room.

She needn't have bothered. Even the thought of his seed, rooted in my belly, made me sick. I gathered my things, stuffed them back into the bag and followed her out.

The señora locked the door behind me. Outside I stood for a moment on the spot where I had last seen my father. His face, my promise. How wrong it had turned out. I turned away and walked to the corner and sounded out the street sign. It still said "Alcalá." Nothing had changed. And everything had changed.

I crossed the street and walked to the park. The morning air was cold. I pulled my rebozo around my shoulders and walked to the market. It was the only place that reminded me of home. Indians, my own people, were there. Someone would help me. In one of the passageways a woman with long gray braids arranged red tomatoes, green tomatillos and white onions. I smiled at her and she smiled back.

"I'm looking for work," I said hopefully. "Do you need help with your stand?"

She shook her head and waved me on. "You won't find work here."

I turned to the woman next to her. She had filled a whole bucket with figs and piled neat rows of pineapples next to oranges. "I will work very hard for you. You won't have to pay me much."

She shook her head and went on with her work.

I walked down all the passages, asking each person if they needed help. "You won't even have to pay me," I began saying. "I just need a little food."

But they looked at my belly and shook their head and waved me on.

I left the market and went to the store I had seen that first day.

"No beggars!" the owner yelled as soon as I had entered.

I stopped in the doorway. "I'm no beggar. I'm looking for work."

He sneered. "Get out. There's no work here for an Indian."

By late afternoon my legs were wobbly and didn't want to walk anymore. I reached into my pocket and counted my money. There was enough to buy some tortillas and maybe some beans, too. I asked a girl on the street if there was someplace nearby where I could eat and she pointed and said there was a market two blocks down.

Inside the market there were shops with huge slabs of meat. Some hung from hooks on the ceiling and some were in metal counters that had windows. The whole place smelled of meat and wetness. Everywhere I looked there was meat. I shuddered.

I turned away from the meat counters. Near the door there were a lot of counters where people sat bunched together eating their dinner. Behind the grill cooks watched thin slices of meat, stirred big pots of beans, turned onions and stacked tortillas inside squares of brown paper. I sat down and studied the sign to see what I could buy. A bowl of beans and a stack of tortillas.

A man put his hands on the counter in front of me and his face in mine. "Fancy place for an Indian."

I didn't understand.

He gestured with his chin.

I looked around the stall.

His face was in mine. "Mestizos here. No Indians."

"Can I please eat here?" I shrank before his size, almost afraid to ask the question.

He stood up, seeming taller and more menacing. "Pay up first!"

I reached into my pocket and pulled out my coins, counted them carefully and put them one by one into his outstretched hand. He counted them again, tossed them into a cash box, and gestured to one of the cooks. Moments later the cook set a bowl of steaming brown beans and a stack of tortillas in front of me. "Don't take too long, Indian girl."

Chapter Eight

In the next week I walked every street in Santa María. I stopped at every shop and asked for work and I even knocked on some doors, but everywhere I went the answer was the same. "You're no good for doing anything."

I didn't say anything, but I knew they were wrong. I was good for doing many things. In my village I was good for changing sounds into letters and letters into sounds. I was good for knowing when the chickens were hungry and when they had eaten so many bugs they didn't need kernels from my hands. But that was a long time ago and I was having a hard time remembering why those things were important.

In the city I had learned to scrub bathrooms and wash sheets and sew on buttons, but they didn't know that. Now I was learning to hold out my hand and accept money from strangers. I was good for doing a lot of things.

The pain that morning was the worst I had ever felt. I didn't sit on the sidewalk to beg. I stayed under the tree. Again and again the pains came, one after another. There must have been a very bad wind in the night to bring such terrible pains. Sweat began running down my cheeks. Sweat and tears mixed together. I held my belly and braced myself against the tree while I tried to stand. Suddenly I felt something wet between my legs. "I'm dying," I cried out.

"Niña!" I looked up to see a woman bending down over me. She held out a hand to steady me. "This baby is coming now!"

"What—how?" I couldn't finish the sentence.

She bent down and told me I should squat, half-standing, half-sitting, my back against the tree. She helped me lower myself. "Yes, yes, that is good. Like that. Now it will come quickly." She put her bundles down and knelt beside me.

The pain became bigger than I was. Suddenly I had to push.

"Yes, that's it, push, push harder. It'll be over soon," she said. I did as she said. I pushed and cried and pushed and cried. She stood up and held me by the shoulders. Then she knelt and reached under my skirt. I felt something come out. "Push again, child. Hard. You're almost done."

I pushed and felt her pull something out of me. She was right. It was all over. I slumped down and leaned back against the tree. I lifted a corner of my skirt and wiped my face. I didn't know what had happened, but I never wanted it to happen again.

"Here she is."

I looked up. The woman held up a baby. It was tiny and wet and covered with bloody white splotches. She wiped its face with her rebozo and held it out to me. "Do you have something to wrap her in?"

I recoiled. "I don't want it."

"Of course you do." She smiled, then looked worried. She blew into the baby's mouth and patted it on its back. "She's not breathing." She patted the baby again, harder this time. "I'm not a midwife. If she doesn't breathe, I won't know what to do."

She began to rub the baby's chest and talk to it. "Come on, baby girl, breathe. Fill your lungs. Give us a good cry now." She stopped talking, put her ear to the baby's chest and waited. Finally she sighed. "Ah, thank God. She's breathing now."

The baby let out a yell. Its hands grasped the air and turned into little fists, its face opened into a wide, crying mouth, its head jerked from side to side as if it were searching for something.

Its cries terrified me. They sounded urgent, panicky. I looked first at the baby then at the woman. "What is the matter with it?"

"It's what babies do. It shows they're alive." She patted the baby and then reached into her pocket and pulled out a rubber band. "She's probably cold." She tied the rubber band around the long cord that was attached to the baby, then reached into her pocket, pulled out a small knife and cut a thick cord that went right into her stomach.

I winced. "Did you kill it?"

She laughed. "No, child." She held the squirming baby with one hand and fumbled through her bag with the other. "Now we need something to wrap her in. I don't have anything but paper." She looked up. "Do you have a blanket?"

I shook my head.

"A pillowcase? Any clothes? Nothing?"

I reached into my bag and pulled out the cloth with the embroidered flowers I had brought from home. "Only this."

She took the cloth and wiped the baby's face. "What a pretty cloth. She'll like it, I'm sure." She wrapped it tightly around the baby and held the bundle out to me. "Do you know how to care for a baby?"

I shook my head. I had seen babies, but not as tiny as this one. In my village women who had babies stayed indoors until one moon had passed. Nobody ever told me what they did. I looked at the tiny face in her arms. "I don't want it."

The woman stood up and looked around. "Do you have family?"

I shook my head.

"Are you working somewhere?"

"No."

She handed the baby to me. "Wrap her inside your rebozo."

The world tilted crazily. I reached out for it, but the bundle blurred and my arms lacked the strength to grasp her. I fumbled with my shawl. "How?"

"Like this." She bent down, opened the shawl, arranged the baby in my arms and covered her up.

Suddenly another warm wetness oozed from between my legs. I grabbed onto her arm. "I'm dying for sure, now."

She smiled and shook her head. "No, it's normal. Relax." I watched, horrified, as she removed a bloody mass from beneath my skirt and wrapped it in a piece of newspaper. "Wait here. Let me see what I can do. I'll come back later." She stood up and turned to go, then turned back. "Keep her next to you so she'll stay warm."

I wasn't sure how I felt about holding this baby I didn't want. It was too intimate, touching and being touched like that.

I called to her as she walked away. "You won't forget, will you?" I don't think she heard me. "I'll wait here until you come back," I cried out. "My father said he'd come back, but he came too late."

She hurried toward the street, market bag in her hand.

The people on the street blurred into a mass of color. Micaela and I were at the river, laughing.

"Bet I can carry more water than you can," she called.

I splashed her. "Bet you can't."

We put our jugs into the water and filled them to the brim, then hoisted them onto our heads, still giggling, and made our way back to our houses. We stopped at the doorway of my house and my mother came out.

She reached out to take the heavy jug from me and gasped. "There's no water here. It's empty."

I shook my head. "But that's impossible. I didn't spill any of it."

My mother looked at me with disgust. She spit. "Bad girl!"

The sun was directly overhead. I looked down at the tiny face in my arms. It had skin the color of mine and hair as dark as mine, but I knew this couldn't be my baby because of la Virgen. My mother had several babies before me, and all of them died. Then she prayed to la Virgen and Our Lady told her that she would send her a special baby. Then I was born. That's why my mother named me Rosa, because I had come straight from the arms of Our Lady. But I hadn't asked la Virgen for a baby and I didn't want this one.

Chapter Nine

I stayed under the tree all afternoon, drifting in and out of sleep. It was a good tree with wide branches and broad leaves. I thought I saw my father walk past on the sidewalk. He wore his best city clothes, a poncho embroidered with flowers and the hat with the colored ribbons that streamed out in all directions, like the first rays of the sun in the morning. He saw me and came running over to fetch me.

He reached down to pull me up, but my body refused to move. My father's outstretched hand slipped slowly from my grasp. Little by little I became aware of the hard ground beneath me, the rough tree bark against my cheek, and that I was alone with a baby I didn't want.

Sometime that day a boy came by on his bicycle. He was younger than me. His red plaid shirt was half in and half out of his patched pants. He had nice eyes. He stared, riding past several times before he spoke. "What's wrong with you?"

"A baby came out of me while I was sitting under the tree and now I'm taking care of it," I said. I held out the bundle in my arms. "Do you want it?"

He scowled. "No, what would I do with a baby?"

I shrugged. "I don't know." I looked past him. "I don't know what to do with a baby, either. I just want to sleep. It's not mine—I didn't ask for it."

He nodded. "Oh."

He pedaled off, but came back a short while later with a soft drink and a roll. He got off his bike and walked toward me. "Do you want something to eat?"

I nodded. "Yes."

He sat down on the grass beside me and held out the roll and the drink. "My sister had a baby."

I bit into the roll and chewed, suddenly very hungry.

He picked a blade of grass and twirled it between his fingers. "Do you have a family?"

I shook my head and bit off another piece of the roll, wetting it unexpectedly with my tears.

"My sister's baby died."

Instinctively I pulled the baby close to my chest.

"It got sick."

I shuddered, peeled back the cloth with my flowers and peered into the sleeping face. I didn't want it, but I didn't want it to die, either. What if I left it here in the park or on the steps of a church? Then I wouldn't have to know what happened to it. I'd leave it on the doorstep and walk away…just like my father had. Suddenly I felt sick. I looked at the tiny person sleeping in my arms, so trusting. "This baby isn't going to die."

He leaned forward and peered into her face. "How do you know?"

"Because I don't want her to." My own words terrified me. What was I agreeing to?

He nodded. "Oh."

"It's not good to be alone." I ran my fingers lightly across her cheek and watched her mouth pucker and her eyes start to open. "I had a best friend once. Her name was Micaela."

"I've never had a best friend." He stood up and picked up his bicycle. "I have to go now." He shuffled uneasily. "Are you all right?"

"No." I looked into his eyes and searched for an answer. "What do you do when you're afraid?"

He studied his feet, kicked the dirt and looked up. "I get into a fight."

"Oh."

He shrugged, turned away and mounted the bicycle and pedaled toward the street.

I was alone again, with the overwhelming task of caring for a baby.

I didn't know what to do or how to do it. What if I did something wrong and she died? I had done plenty wrong before. I had been careless with the water, forgotten to feed the chickens and had lied to my grandmother. Taking care of a baby was too much to even think about.

The giddiness that comes with fear swept over me. When I woke up, I was looking up into the face of the woman who had found the baby inside me. She bent over me and lifted the baby out of my rebozo.

I looked up at her. "She's still breathing."

She patted the baby on its bottom and murmured soft sounds in her ear. "Have you fed her?"

I shook my head. The woman hadn't said to feed her.

"Do you know how?"

I shook my head again. Tears came to my eyes. "No."

She held the bundle in her arms and began to rock her. "I spoke to the señora where I work. She's a good woman. I told her you were my niece. I told her you didn't have anyplace to go. She said you could stay with us for a while—until you find work."

I tried to stand up, but my knees buckled and I fell against the tree trunk and slid back to the ground.

She reached for my arm. "Easy now, child. Easy."

I leaned against the tree for support and pulled myself to my feet. The world moved like water for a moment, and then found its equilibrium.

"My name is Angelina," the woman said. "I've been the cook in the señora's house for fifteen years." She glanced at me. "That's probably longer than you've been on this earth."

"Yes."

She held the baby in one arm, and put the other around me. "We'll walk slowly, it's not far. What are you going to call her?"

I stared at her blankly. I hadn't asked for this baby. Did I have to name her? It wasn't like when I named my chickens. I knew I was responsible for them, but this, this was something that made no sense at all.

She led me to the edge of the park. "You have to name her." She spoke with a soothing authority.

I wanted to believe her. I wanted to cling to her and her words and empty my tears into her apron. We walked down the steps out of the park to the sidewalk. "Why?"

"So we can take her to be baptized."

"Oh." I thought for a moment. I had wrapped her in my embroidered flowers. The cloth I had come to the city to sell so that my parents wouldn't argue and my father wouldn't have to work so hard. The cloth of my innocence, when I didn't know parents sold their own children. "Flor," I said. "Flower."

Chapter Ten

"**R**osa, your baby is crying. I think she's hungry." Angelina's voice wafted up through the laughter in the kitchen to the rooftop where I was washing clothes.

"Coming." I wrung out the sheet, shook it and threw it across the line. I imagined the laughter wrapping itself in the sheets and the sweet dreams it would give.

"This child is going to be a singer someday. What a voice!" she called.

I straightened the sheet out on the line, fastened a pin at either end and hurried down stairs to the kitchen where a radio blared happy music. The sixth of January was Reyes, Three Kings Day, and we had a lot to do. The brightly lit kitchen made the day seem warmer than it was. Berta, the maid, sat at a small table trimming the prickly thorns from the nopales. A pot of beans bubbled quietly on the stove and just-made tamales, tied in banana leaves and ready to be steamed, lay mounded on a large platter. I had stepped out of a nightmare and into a dream.

Angelina made cooing noises to the bundle in her arms. "I've changed her diaper already." She held her out to me. "I'm going to the bakery to fetch a rosca. When you're finished feeding her, I need some help preparing for the festivities."

I took the baby and went into the small room where Berta had made a pallet on the floor for me. I sat down, opened the uniform and put her mouth to my nipple the way Angelina had showed me. It was scary, being responsible for a baby. She was so tiny. So fragile. I wanted so much to protect her.

"Flor," I whispered. "It's good here at the señora's house. They like us." I touched her cheek with my finger and swallowed hard. "I hope we can stay."

She reached for my finger and wrapped her hand around it as if to say, "I hope so, too."

I looked into the eyes of my little dark-haired baby. I didn't know newborn babies had a smell of their own, but I loved it. So clean and sweet. I ran my fingers across her cheeks and down her arms. I had never felt skin that soft. "You and the new sun were born at the same time of the year, did you know that?"

She looked at me as though she understood.

I moved her plump little hand back and forth with my finger. "It's a new year and a new life."

Flor fell asleep as soon as her belly was full. I laid her on the pallet and tiptoed out. Berta pointed to a mound of potatoes that needed peeling and a couple of onions waiting to be chopped. "Angelina says we have to prove to the señora that you are earning your keep," she said.

Angelina was like a mother to me. In this house Angelina and Berta were my only family. I hoped the señora would see how hard I worked and let me stay.

Minutes later Angelina burst through the back door, carrying a large package tied with string. "You wouldn't believe the people in the bakery. Everybody wanting a rosca today. I don't know why they all waited until the last minute."

Berta winked at me. "Imagine that."

Angelina ignored Berta's comment and my giggles and laid the package on the kitchen table.

Berta stood up from the table with the bowl of nopales. "These are ready to cut, Rosa. Neat little squares, please." Then to no one in particular she said, "I wonder who will get the niño?"

Angelina let out a deep sigh. "I hope it's not the señora again this year. I've had enough of parties for now." She looked around the kitchen. "Those potatoes ready yet?"

I reached for a knife. "Almost."

After we finished with the lunch dishes, Berta bathed Flor in the kitchen sink. I stood by her side and watched. It seemed very difficult because Flor couldn't sit by herself and unless someone held her, she slumped over.

"Don't you want to bathe her today?" Berta asked.

I shook my head and took a step back. "No! She's too little. I'm afraid she'll slide out of my hands and drown." The idea terrified me.

She smiled. "She won't. And if she does, you can catch her." She glanced to her side, where I stood hesitantly. "You have to learn, sooner or later."

I shook my head, harder this time. "No, I can't. I don't know how."

"Rosa, you're too afraid of her. Stop being so afraid. She's a strong girl." She glanced up at me. "Like you."

That evening everybody in the household ate their fill of tamales. Sweet tamales, spicy ones, some filled with chicken and mole sauce, others with pork, still others with squash blossoms and cheese. We ate until our bellies begged us to stop.

On the stove a large pot of milk warmed, making the entire kitchen smell sweet and homey. Berta stood in front of the stove, breaking off pieces of dark cinnamon-flavored chocolate and dropping them into the milk. When she finished, she picked up the carved wooden molinillo and twirled it between her hands until the chocolate was foamy.

"Once when his flowers sold well my father bought us some chocolate," I said. "My mother mixed it with hot water and a little goat's milk. She beat it just like that until it was foamy and then she poured it into our bowls and we sat there, my grandmother, my parents and I, like the four bearers of the earth, drinking the nectar of the gods and remembering that we were in the center of the universe." I looked down, suddenly embarrassed.

For a moment no one said anything. Then Angelina asked, "Why don't you go home, Rosa?"

"That was a long time ago," I said, uncomfortable at having spoken. "Before the sky fell in." Before the dishonor.

"Angelina, we're ready for the rosca," the señora called.

I was glad for the interruption. Berta and I filled a large pitcher with the hot chocolate mixture, which she took in to the dining room while Angelina slid the rosca onto a platter and set it down in front of the señora. Strips of candied fruit lay across the top, guarding the secret whereabouts of the niño inside. The three of us stood by the table, waiting excitedly to see who would get the little plastic doll. The señora cut into the fresh cake and put a slice onto a plate, which she passed to her husband. Then two more slices, which she passed to her children. Another for the aunt and still no niño. In all six slices were cut and still no sign of the niño.

We giggled with discomfort. It wouldn't do for one of us to get the doll that represented the Christ child. We couldn't give a party in its honor.

Angelina rested her hands across her stomach and smiled when the señora glanced up. "You'll just have to keep eating, señora."

The señora shook her head, picked up a fork and delicately probed the rest of the cake. "Nothing here," she said, even when the fork refused to go in. She reached for the knife, cut out the stubborn piece and handed it to Angelina. "Provecho."

Angelina bowed her head and tried to cover the embarrassment on her face. "No, señora, I couldn't," she said, reaching out to take the plate.

The señora smiled. "Couldn't what? Take an extra day off?"

Angelina bowed her head again. "Thank you, señora."

The señora lifted the platter off the table and handed it to Berta. "Take this into the kitchen. You know it doesn't keep well."

We dipped pieces of rosca into steaming cups of hot chocolate and talked until well into the night. Even the Christ child didn't enjoy himself more than we did that evening.

Two evenings later the señora came into the kitchen. Dinner was over, the dishes had been washed, Christmas parties were behind us and the new year had begun. Everything was in order except that Berta had eaten too much. Angelina prepared an herbal tea she was making us drink.

The señora poured herself a glass of water from the large bottle. "Rosa, have you found work yet?"

Her question riddled me with fear. I lowered my head and stared at the floor. "Not yet, señora. Please let us stay a little longer."

Angelina put her hand on my shoulder. "The baby's too small yet. She really hasn't had time to look." She glanced sideways at Berta and then at me. "She can go out tomorrow if it's not too cold. We can watch the baby for a while in the morning, can't we, Berta?"

Berta looked at the señora for an answer.

The señora studied me for a second, and then nodded. "I hope you can find work soon." She looked at Angelina, whose hand rested protectively on my shoulder. "I know she's your niece, and she's helping, but she really needs to find work in some other house." The señora looked back at me. "We like having you, Rosa, but we just can't afford it right now. I'm sure you understand."

I tried to stop the tears that filled my eyes, but she must have noticed them in spite of my efforts. "You knew your stay here was only temporary."

"Yes, señora, I knew."

The next day I went out as soon as the breakfast dishes were done. It was too cold for a baby, but midmorning I went back to feed her and take her with me so that Angelina and Berta could finish preparing lunch. I wrapped her securely in my rebozo and moved, first from the nearby streets and then further and further away from the house I wanted to call home. None of the señoras I spoke with wanted to hire a girl with a baby. I returned to Angelina's house late in the afternoon.

"Any luck?" Berta asked.

"They all say the same thing," I said, patting the sleeping bundle in my arms. "Leave the baby with your mother. Then come talk to me."

Berta and Angelina exchanged knowing glances. "You haven't been home, have you?"

I studied the beans on my plate. "No."

Every morning for the next week I went out. And every afternoon I reported the same thing. At week's end I still had not found work. I didn't tell them how afraid I was that someone would say yes. How I dreaded that past their open door lay a hell as bad as the one I had just left.

At the end of January Flor turned one month old. She was healthy and happy and so was I. We were both eating well and we were flourishing, surrounded by people who cared about us. It was paradise. But, as I already knew, paradise doesn't last.

The house seemed empty now that the holidays were over. The children had gone back to school and just the señora and her husband remained. Two of them and three of us. I knew it couldn't last, but I hoped anyway.

The señora came into the kitchen that afternoon while we were drying the lunch dishes. "Rosa," she began, "You're a nice girl, and very helpful around the house. I can't deny it." She looked around the kitchen.

I hoped she would say that it had never been cleaner, that the meals had never been more delicious and that she had never been more satisfied, but I knew that was not what she had come to say.

She smiled sympathetically. "But it's time for you to find work elsewhere."

"Please, señora, you don't have to pay me."

The stern look on her face told me there was little chance of changing her mind. "I'm sure you'll find something. There's always somebody looking for a maid."

I washed my uniforms and sheets and hung them on the clothesline to dry. I swept the room we shared with Berta, bathed, and tried not to cry while Angelina combed my wet hair back from my face. Her touch was soft and so were her words. I took my blue blouse out of the armoire. I tried to remember what it felt like to fall into eternity through that blouse, but the memories wouldn't come. I put on the skirt from Saint John the Baptist and wound the belt that carried my grandmother's words, now silenced by dishonor, around my waist.

I folded the clean cloths Angelina had given me and tucked my baby inside my rebozo.

"Where will you go?" she asked.

I shrugged. "No one wants a girl with a baby."

Berta tucked a twenty-peso bill and a couple of warm rolls in my rebozo. "Perhaps you can work in a store."

I nodded. "Yes, perhaps." No Indian girl ever worked in a store. She knew that.

Angelina ran her hand down my cheek. "Are you sure you don't want to go to your village? I'll give you enough money for the bus."

I nodded. "Yes, I'm sure."

She walked me to the door and hugged me. "Well, come see me if you need anything."

I nodded. "I will," I said. But I knew I wouldn't.

Chapter Eleven

My grandmother always said everything had a soul. She said the soul was a spark of the fire that burned in the sun. I wasn't connected to the sun anymore. I wandered, lost and adrift.

The first night we stayed in a park. The cold burned so intensely I hardly slept at all. I had to find a place for us.

That afternoon orange light cast purple shadows in the streets. The Underworld beckoned to the sun on the far side of the mountain, and soon cold and darkness would consume the city. I walked along a mostly empty sidewalk, bent over to ward off the slicing cold. Shopkeepers were closing up for the day and all around me protective gates slammed into place, saying "Keep out."

Four blocks from the market I found an abandoned, half-built building. The door and windows were boarded up. I walked past several times, checking to see that no one was using it and that no watchman stood guard. Then I stopped and peered inside. Half-empty sacks of concrete and piles of garbage lay strewn about. Satisfied that we would be safe, I pushed past the boarded up doorway. Several small birds fluttered high in the corners. The building had a roof, which was good, because sometimes the rains came in the winter months. Not hard or long, but cold enough to put frost on the trees. For all that it lacked, it was better than sleeping in the park. I pulled back the corner of my rebozo and peered into the eyes of my baby.

"Flor, this is our new home." My words bounced off the hard walls.

Dust particles hung suspended in the late afternoon air, unsure where they belonged. "These are the walls, and over there is the door and if we are very careful, we can come in and out without getting any splinters in our fingers." She smiled and grabbed at my hand.

"We'll sleep here tonight and in the morning we'll find a sunny place to sit and warm up. We will ask people for money and look for work. Does that seem like a good plan to you?"

She must have thought so, for she made tiny gurgling noises.

That night we settled in as best we could. Concrete floors don't give too much, and after a while I found it easier to sleep sitting up leaning against the corner walls. Sometime during the night a shuffling noise woke me. Boards across the windows denied entrance to the light from the street and the darkness kept its silent secrets. I couldn't tell what the noise was and I wasn't sure what to do—run, or stay still and hope it wasn't a rat.

I made myself as small as I could, huddled in the corner, and tried to breathe quietly. Was it an animal? Had it picked up our scent? Was it baring its teeth, ready to attack? Or had a person—a night watchman, or worse, a policeman, made the noise? Of the two, I didn't know which I feared most, a wild animal or the wrong person.

I strained to decipher the sounds in the dark. My mind saw what my eyes could not. Possums with sharp teeth. Vicious hungry rats. Wild dogs that could tear a person apart. Snakes. Tarantulas. The thought of teeth sinking into my flesh stopped my breath. I held Flor closer to me. The muscles of my body contracted, ready to defend against attack, flinching against prying eyes, sharp teeth or an intrusive beam of light, but nothing came. Hours later the dim gray morning light revealed the noise had not come from an animal, but a boy.

Relieved, I watched him for a while. He lay face down on the cold concrete floor, one arm stretched out under his head, the other under his belly. I couldn't see his face. His blue pants were torn and dirty and his shirt was frayed. I reached out and tapped the sole of his shoe with my foot.

He didn't move.

I stood up. He was dead. He must have died from the cold. I shivered and hugged my baby closer to me. "Flor, we have spent the night with a dead body. That is not a good thing to do. Tonight we must find another place to stay."

I crawled through the jagged boards across the doorway and didn't look back. Death had come too close. I walked to the market and bought a cup of hot chocolate and a roll. The warm cup felt good in my hands. It reminded me of Angelina's house and life.

My baby's muffled cries pushed through the folds of my rebozo. I reached under my blouse and put her to suck. "You cry too faintly," I murmured. "Like me. Are we wrong to want to be here?" I took the last sip of chocolate from my cup and returned it to the counter.

Around me people filed in, bought hot drinks and fresh bread, eggs, tamales, beans, sat down, ate, talked, made plans. Everyone seemed to have a purpose. They were here for a reason, either buying or selling. What were we doing here? What was the sense of this? In my village I had grown up surrounded by meaning, but here I could find no meaning in anything. Were we seeds thrown to the wind, seeds that would never find earth, never find life? What power decided which seeds would flower and which would not? I wanted nothing to do with gods like this.

"Niña!" The shopkeeper snapped. "Take that baby somewhere else. Your dirty face and its cries drive all my customers away!"

"Good!" My angry voice replied. "Then you won't be able to poison them with your food." The anger in my reply surprised me. I grabbed up my roll, went outside and sat down on the curb to eat.

It was no good, trying to hurt another. It didn't make me hurt any the less. I ate my roll and watched people rush by, pushing carts.

White onions, imprisoned in brown burlap bags, took a last peek at the world through small squares. Red tomatoes, packed into crowded boxes, lay passively as they were separated and sold. Green chili peppers rode proudly into the market, ignorant of the fact that soon they would be ground to a pulp. The patrón was right. Everybody used everybody else; everything was a sacrifice.

A man unloaded a tank of gas from a truck, put his hand out and pushed me to one side. "Get out of the way, little girl."

A woman splashed a bucket of water onto the sidewalk behind me.

"I'm cleaning now. You'd better go."

I left, wandered through the streets until I found a church. I don't know which saint it belonged to, but I liked it. Lots of steps led up to the church that sat high on a hill, overlooking the streets below. Around the grounds white sheet tents fluttered in the breeze and underneath vendors, Indians like me, unpacked pretty things to sell.

I sighed. This was where I belonged, here, among my people. I wandered through the passageways, looking at all the pretty things. Blouses, rebozos, hair ribbons, sweaters, blankets. I stopped to touch a blanket. It would feel good on these cold nights.

An Indian face yelled, "Go on, now, niña. You stink! You'll scare my customers away!"

"Go away!" Indian hands shooed me.

I walked away but stopped at another stall. Knives. Hand-carved knives. My father would certainly like that. I stooped to have a better look, but a slew of Indian words and Indian gestures motioned me away. "You're full of lice! Go on, now, get away!"

The words stabbed me in the stomach. It wasn't only their words that drove me away. It was the look in their eyes. The look that said we were no longer the same people made by the same gods.

All afternoon I looked for work. One man laughed and said, "Of what use is an Indian girl with a baby?"

"I'm a hard worker. You'll see."

He sneered. "I can see that. But I don't have that kind of business."

I turned and walked away.

The orange of the afternoon sky had given way to red and the air began to bite with each breath. It was the dark time of the year, when the nights brought frost. People bundled up, walked faster, and lights came on earlier in the shops. I looked for a new place to stay the night. I walked until well past dark, but found only a dumpsite, which I dared not stop in for fear of wild dogs and rats. Only the same empty building presented itself. Unsure of what to do, I walked past it several times. The thought of another night with a dead body sent shivers through me, but the thought of sleeping in the park and hoping no night watchman would find me sent worse feelings. I chose the dead body.

I squeezed past the slats across the doorway and peered around the corner into the room where I had spent the previous night. Darkness had arrived before us, had already settled in and claimed its space. I stood for a moment, then took a deep breath. I didn't notice the stench of a corpse. Either it was frozen or someone had moved it.

Slowly I walked in, feeling my way along the frigid wall to the corner, where I again sank down. Concrete, like the city, was indifferent. I leaned against the hard wall, put my whimpering baby to my breast and fell asleep.

Another shuffling noise woke me during the night. I sat up, opened my eyes and clutched the baby tightly to my chest. A dull thud. Then nothing. I waited. Nothing. No teeth, no flashlight, no attack.

The morning light uncovered the body of the boy again. He still lay face down on the concrete. One arm was still bent under his head, the other lay by his side, almost like the day before. The soles of his shoes were torn and his feet stuck out. His clothes were dirty and torn. It was the same boy I had seen the day before. The dead boy.

I crept to his side and leaned over his body. I wondered if anyone would say a mass for him, or light a candle or even remember him for Los Muertos. I sat, looking at his body, wondering how he had died. Was it from the cold? Or from hunger? Perhaps he had gotten sick. "If you died in my village we would dress you up in your best clothes and clean you and invite your friends to come and visit. We'd put candles around you and flowers, too." I pretended to arrange them around his body. "Like this."

"The priest will be here in a little while, and the shaman, too." I spoke as if he could hear me. "After the priest leaves, the shaman will light the candles and drink aguardiente and call the gods. You'll know when they come because the candles will flicker." I blew softly at one of the imaginary candles. "Then the gods will take you to the Otherworld and you will be happy there." I smiled.

"May you rest in peace," I said. The tips of my fingers grazed his shoulder. He moaned. I jerked my hand back, and scuttled quickly across the floor to the opposite side of the room. My heart thumped wildly.

I uttered a prayer to Saint John the Baptist. "I'm sorry to have interfered," I stammered. "I meant no harm." I glanced at the body on the floor. "Please protect me from the gods of the Underworld and the evil winds." I waited and watched, then prayed again. "Please, hear me, Saint John the Baptist, you are my only hope," I begged.

My grandmother said sometimes the spirit of the dead person did not leave the body for three days. I looked at the body across the room. She said sometimes it needed to grieve, too, just like the people it left behind. I watched for signs of grieving. All it did was moan. Maybe that was what they did. Maybe that's how the spirits of the dead grieved. It sounded sad to me.

Chapter Twelve

Saint John the Baptist must have heard me because he gave me the strength to let this spirit grieve without me. I clutched my baby tight against my chest and dashed out.

All that day I looked for work, and all day I heard the same replies I had heard the day before, until at last the truth made itself known to me: An Indian girl with a baby was good for nothing. I sat down on the sidewalk and stared, but the concrete offered no solution.

That afternoon as the cold crept back into the city, I went into the church with the steps I'd seen before. Perhaps, just this once, the saints would not mind sharing their big house with me. In my village we took turns taking care of the saints. Each year a guardian took them into his house, prepared their festivals and watched over them. I wasn't even going to ask them to watch over me—I just wanted a warm place to sleep where there were no dead bodies.

The church smelled faintly of candle wax and incense. Familiar smells. Vases of bright yellow flowers stood on the altars and intricate carvings in gold, the color of the sun, surrounded each of the saints, as if we were all longing for light in the dark time of the year. People knelt here and there as if an unseen hand had dropped them into the dimly lit sanctuary. Flor and I slipped into the corner of a pew in the back and waited for them to leave. It felt good just to sit in the semi-darkness. Comforting and safe. As the afternoon turned into evening a priest wearing a long black robe made the rounds and closed the doors. He seemed not to notice us.

I waited a while. "Everybody's left, Flor," I whispered. "We'll find a place to hide and you must be very quiet." I put my finger on my mouth and then hers. "Then later we'll come out and sleep on a pew tonight." It seemed like such a good idea I wondered why I hadn't thought of it before.

Behind a wrought iron railing stood a small altar covered in gold. The saint stared ahead, looking past us as if we weren't there. Two fingers of one hand joined in a circle and the other hand rested over her heart. In front of her rows of candles burned in small red glasses, their flickering shadows providing the only movement in the now still church. I slipped past the tall gate and crouched in the corner behind the altar. It was a good place, out of sight and still warm.

A heavy door clanked shut and the lights went out, one by one, until only the light of the flickering candles remained. The empty church now became a silent tomb, where soulless statues receded into the darkness behind racks of smoking candles. Flor whimpered.

"Shh!" I rocked her and patted her bottom.

She whimpered again. Her small voice echoed through the empty darkness. In the distance footsteps faded, stopped and then grew louder. I squeezed my eyes shut. Without warning it was Sunday again and the footsteps were coming from the front door, through the kitchen and into my room. Hard-soled shoes against a cold marble floor. My lower lip began to tremble. Please, no. Sweat bathed my body. The footsteps didn't end when they reached my room. They came closer and closer, got louder and louder. Finally they stopped. I opened my eyes and looked up. Terror, in the guise of two shiny black shoes, planted itself before me.

"Get up, girl!" the voice commanded.

I couldn't get up. I couldn't move. I bit my lip, but tears flowed down my cheeks anyway. Instead I looked down at the floor and wished with all my heart to be invisible.

"Get up!" A strong arm in a black sleeve reached out and pulled me to my feet. "Do you want me to call the authorities?"

I wiped my cheeks with the back of my hand and looked up into the face of the priest. I clutched Flor closer to my chest.

A stern voice exploded out of the darkness. "What are you doing, girl? Why are you hiding in here? Don't you know the saints don't like people to hide in their house?"

Flor cried out.

I shushed her and shook my head at him. "No, I'm sorry, I didn't know that."

He grabbed my arm and marched us toward the door. "Did you come here to steal?"

"No," I whispered. Until now it hadn't occurred to me. What could one steal from a church? Candles? Flowers? Why not? The saints surely didn't need so many. For all I knew, they had gone off like the gods, leaving only the blank stares on their faces.

"If you steal from the house of God, you could spend all eternity in hell!" he said, shoving us out the door and slamming it behind us.

I walked out into the cold night air, empty except for the cries of a small baby. All eternity in hell. I wondered if he had any idea what it was like, this hell he threatened. I could have told him.

I descended the steps into the city. Outside the streets were quiet. People scurried along the sidewalks, going home to a warm fireplace like the one at Angelina's house. There we often sat in the kitchen until late in the evenings to keep warm. We put water on to boil to soak the beans for cooking the next day, but sometimes if it was really cold, we pretended to forget about it and we let the water boil much longer than it needed to. I wished I could go home to Angelina's house.

Flor was cold, hungry and wet. I walked the nearly deserted streets, looking for a fire in a vacant lot, or an elote vendor or someone selling hot drinks, imagining how good the fire would feel. A warm place to sit, to change her, to feed her. I walked for a long time, looking for something, anything to take away the intense cold, but the city had turned inside for the night.

The sound of my own footsteps led me back to the empty building. Like the night before, I stopped at the entrance and sniffed the air for the smell of corpse, but I was in luck. It was too cold for a corpse to rot. I settled into my corner and felt the cold seep into my flesh and settle into my bones. I shivered, put Flor to my breast and fell asleep.

The next morning the body lay in the same place, but in a different position. This time it was curled up with its knees to its chest. My grandmother said in the old days that was the way bodies were put into the earth. But when the priest came he said his god didn't like people to sit in the earth. They had to lie down instead. I don't know why it made any difference, but that's the way we did it after that. If this body liked the old ways, then his wishes had to be respected.

If I were going to light candles for him, I wanted to see who he was. I knelt beside him, careful not to touch, and peered into his face. He was just a boy, no older than I. His face was dark from not being washed, and something about him looked familiar.

I gasped. It was the boy from the festival—the one who had bought me a drink. The one who said my eyes sparkled like sunlight and who wanted to be my friend. The one who said my shoes had fireworks in them. I pulled away and sat up. It was too much. Too unfair. What about his dream of working hard and saving his money to build a house with two rooms and a roof? Where would that dream live, now that he was dead? Who would carry it for him? Who would bring it forth? It wasn't just the boy that had died; it was all that he stood for.

I looked at his body, all alone, with no family to grieve for him. I decided then that I would light candles for him, even if I had to steal them from a church. I leaned closer and looked into his face. "I will remember you," I whispered. "Even if I am the only one."

His hair, cut in jagged chunks, stood out in all angles from his face. I sat back and ran my fingers through my own hair. It felt coarse and gritty, like his looked. Without warning his eyes opened. The fright of seeing the dead spring to life stopped my heart. I fell back, struck with panic. "Please don't hurt me," I stammered. "I only wanted to remember your face."

He sat up and rubbed his eyes. "What's wrong with my face?"

"Nothing." I tilted my head and looked at him. I had never spoken with a dead person before, but my grandmother had done it all the time. She said it was just like speaking to a live person. "How long have you been dead?"

He looked surprised. "How long do you think?"

I looked him over carefully. "The cold has preserved you well." His body was thin, but not yet stiff. The pale color in his face might have been from dust and dirt, but it didn't yet reflect the colorless hue of a corpse.

He cocked his head to one side. "And you, how long have you been dead?"

I shook my head. "I'm not dead. I have a baby." I opened my rebozo.

He leaned toward me and looked, then sat back. "Are you hungry?"

I nodded.

"So am I. Do you have any money?"

I reached inside my blouse and pulled out a five-peso note. It was all I had left. I showed it to him.

He looked, but did not reach to take it. "If you'll buy me something to eat, I'll give the money back to you as soon as the patrón pays me."

I nodded, but wondered how he would do that from the spirit world. "How soon will you leave?" I asked.

He looked perplexed.

"For the spirit world."

He grinned and shook his head. "Not for a long time."

I believed him. A spark in his eyes reminded me of something. I couldn't remember what it was.

Chapter Thirteen

In the daytime Flor and I sat on the sidewalk near a busy supermarket. An automatic door on my right took people in empty-handed and spit them back out later carrying lots of little white plastic bags stuffed with daily necessities. A bicycle rack stood behind me, and cars parked directly in front. It was a good place. Almost everybody had to walk by me to go inside. When they did, I held out my hand.

At first I looked at the people who gave me money, and thanked them, but then I noticed they didn't look back. I think they wanted to pretend I wasn't there. Like the señoras who pretended not to know what their husbands were doing.

I couldn't blame them. I pretended I wasn't sitting on the street begging for enough money to stay alive. I pretended that it didn't matter that I had stopped being a real person or that my life depended on the whims of a stranger. We all pretended.

After I realized no one was ever going to look at me, or ask me how it had come to that, I stopped caring that it had, or that they didn't care. Instead, I stared into the traffic. When a pair of shoes approached, I held out my hand. Sometimes a coin would drop into it, sometimes not. No one ever touched me and no one ever spoke. Sometimes the shoes approached, then stepped down into the street, and then stepped back on the sidewalk on the other side.

The boy and I pretended, too. In the evenings we met in the empty building, but now we called it our house. Our big house.

To me it was just a big, cold, empty space, but to him, it was proof of his dream. One evening he leaned against the wall, his hands resting on his knees. "I'm going to build a house as big as this some day, you'll see."

I knew he would, too. He believed it so much, I knew that house had to come to him, just like when the gods had to come when my grandmother prayed enough.

"My house is going to have two rooms and a roof." He stood up and turned around in the middle of the room, his arms flung out as if we were already there. "And it's going to have furniture, too."

"What kind of furniture—a table?" I knew he was seeing his house in the spirit world because there he had already built it. He was seeing it there and birthing it into this world.

He nodded. "With chairs. And shelves. And a window. Maybe two."

He believed so strongly in that house that I could see it too. It was his strength that forced the question out of me. "What's your name?" To name something was powerful magic. It brought the thing you named into being—that's why you had to be so careful with your words.

"Martín." He grinned. "And yours?"

The skin on my face prickled. I looked down at the floor. "Rosa." The breath flowed out of me and it was done. We existed. We were real. At least to each other.

We played lots of games at our house. Sometimes we pretended we were king and queen and that Flor was the princess. We pretended we had all sorts of food to eat like tamales, guavas, frijoles, watermelon and peaches and juicy ripe mangos. And all the tortillas our bellies could hold. We licked our hands, laughing and pretending they were sticky with mango juice. Sometimes we pretended our fingers burned, not from the cold, but from unwrapping steaming tamales, and we made a game of tossing them back and forth to each other. Sometimes I sliced a make-believe watermelon and we spit make-believe seeds at imaginary targets.

Sometimes we pretended everyone in the whole world had died and we were the only survivors. "My grandmother said that happened once," I said.

Martín looked at me with disbelief. "No, really? The whole world?"

I nodded and went on. "She said the gods got mad because nobody remembered them and so they sent a great flood and everybody drowned."

Martín thought about it for a moment. "Then I guess we will have to be careful to remember the gods and talk about them often."

I turned away. "The gods in my village left. They found a place they liked better, so I don't talk to them anymore," I said. "I only talk to the saints."

Martín propped one knee up and rested his arm on it. "The saints belong to the city people, not to us."

I shrugged. "If there are any gods in the city, they have forgotten us. They don't love us anymore."

Martín stared off into the distance. When he finally spoke, his voice sounded far away. "Then maybe we have to love us."

His words startled me. "Do you think we can do that?"

He nodded. "Yes, I think it's all right."

A strange sensation filled my belly. Like I had finally gotten enough to eat.

That Friday after I had eaten a bowl of beans and some tortillas, I had some coins left over. I saved them and before long I had saved enough to buy a candle. I stopped in the market at the end of the day and bought a pretty white candle. It had to be white—for her. That evening when Martín came, he said he wanted to remember the gods, even though I didn't believe in them.

"Just in case you change your mind someday," he said. An annoying grin covered his face.

We cut some low pine branches from a tree in the park, brought them back and spread them on the floor. Martin set the candle in the middle, just like my grandmother used to do when she called in the gods.

"My grandmother was a healer."

Martín's eyes flickered with interest.

"I used to go with her sometimes," I said. "We spread pine needles on the floor of the church, just like this." I gestured at the floor. "And then we lit lots of little candles and set them into the hot wax so they wouldn't fall over." I could see her as clearly as if were happening right now. I swallowed and looked up at Martín.

"Then what?"

"Then my grandmother would light the copal resin and begin to call in the gods. She said they couldn't resist the sweet smell so they always came." I smiled at Martín. "They did, too." I stared, remembering. "I set the four drinks in front of her—red, white, yellow and black—one for each of the directions. And she sang their songs." I stopped. "I didn't mean to talk so much."

He smiled. "It's good, go on."

I turned my face away. "But that's just superstition. We live in the city now. Besides, I don't believe in the gods anymore. I told you that."

Martín stared silently into the candle flame. Finally he said, "I still believe in them."

"Then we'll do this for you."

We watched the candle burn and the light flicker. When the candle burned down to the floor, it caught the pine needles on fire. Suddenly the room filled with light, and loud popping noises came from everywhere, and the room filled with a wonderful aroma.

Martín jumped up and began to dance around the room, waving his hat and stomping his feet. "Yahoo!" he yelled. "All the gods in creation must be here tonight. What a celebration!"

The noise frightened Flor and she began to cry. I shushed her and tried to explain to her that it was all right. As quickly as it began, the noise and the light disappeared, and we were left with only a tiny light and a room filled with the delicious scent of pine boughs.

A smile covered Martín's face. "Wow! That was just like we used to do it at home." His voice wavered and the floor suddenly became interesting. "Doesn't it make you want to go back home, Rosa? To be with your family?"

I turned my head away.

In the semi-darkness Martin crawled across the room and crouched before me. He spoke barely above a whisper. "They love you." He paused before finishing his sentence. " How could they not? Just like the gods still love you."

I shook my head and looked at the floor. I wanted to believe him. With my whole heart I wanted to believe him. But that belief didn't live in me.

Martín didn't always have all the answers. The next night we didn't pretend anything because he didn't come back until very late. When he did, he smelled awful and acted very strange. I think he was drunk. I had seen men in our village that had drunk too much aguardiente and he had the same strange look in his eyes as they did. Once my father had pulled me close to him and put his hands over my eyes so I wouldn't see them, but I had already looked.

Martín didn't say anything, but his eyes were not right. They were full of anger. He pulled a match from his pocket, lit a small candle and set it on the floor between us.

There was a tremor in his voice. "Every day the patrón pours aguardiente in my soda. He says it will make me work better, so I drink it," he said. "I don't like it, but I do it."

"That's not bad." I knelt down in front of him.

The tiny flame struggled hard to warm the space around us. It flickered and swayed, but the cold stood its ground.

He raised his knee and rested his elbow on it and wiped his face with the collar of his torn shirt. "Then today, when it was time to pay me for the week, he said I had drunk all my pay." His voice quivered. "He didn't pay me!"

I reached past the candle to touch his hand, but pulled back and offered my words instead. "He didn't give you any money?"

Martín shook his head and pulled an empty whiskey bottle out of his pocket. "He gave me this and said it was all that was left of my pay."

The shadow of his arm and the bottle filled the entire wall. The shadow heaved, trembled and then slumped into a heap. Martín began to sob. "Nothing! He paid me nothing! A whole week I worked—for nothing!"

I sat while he cried.

A long while passed until he sat up. He wiped his face on his sleeve. I waited.

He slammed his fist into his hand. "I got back at him."

"What did you do?"

He stared into the flame. "I took the bottle and drank what was left of it." Then he looked up at me and his eyes flashed a crazed look. "Then, when he was up front, locking up, I stole from him."

"You stole?" I could see an idea forming in his mind.

"It was easy." He paused, smiling to himself. "Maybe I'll do it again."

"What will he do if he catches you?" In my village nobody stole—at least not very often. I almost stole something from the patrón. I was glad I hadn't.

"He's not going to catch me." He looked at me. "You'll see. If he doesn't pay me, I'll just take what he owes me."

I could see the determined look on his face and I knew he meant what he said. After that night he began to change, little by little. It was as if the city were slowly swallowing him. His heart became hard and all the things that mattered so much before didn't matter at all anymore. Maybe he just got tired. Tired of believing when there was nothing to believe in.

Chapter Fourteen

No one in the city used the real calendar, where every day was a god, so no one knew about the five bad luck days. I could feel something bad coming and I was frightened.

"You shouldn't go out tonight. It's not safe."

Martín shrugged me off. "That's village talk. We're in the city now. The city has its own rules." He stood up and slicked back his hair with his hand. "Special days don't live in the city, you should know that."

Martín quit talking about the house he was going to build and we hardly played pretend games except once in a while. I think it began that first time the patrón didn't pay him. It was like the sky started falling down around him the way it had fallen around me. I felt bad for him, because there was nothing I could say. I knew the gods were capricious, and I knew they had stopped taking care of us a long time ago, but he didn't and that's why he hurt now.

For days he had come back to our big house with the smell of alcohol on his breath. When I asked him if he had eaten, he would answer angrily and then fall asleep.

Tonight I watched him prepare to go out and shook my head. "I don't believe in the gods, but you do. You said the gods are everywhere, even in the city."

"I was wrong."

Memories of dried cornstalks flooded my mind. My parents had protected me against the harshness of life. I hadn't understood then that too much heat could reduce a plump golden kernel into colorless dust. Or that a person could die slowly from the inside out. "The patrón didn't pay you again for the week, did he?"

"No." He turned when he reached the doorway.

"Why don't you find some other work?"

Martín scuffed the dust on the floor. "He says I have a contract with him. If I don't show up, he'll send the police."

He looked up from his shoe. "I'll be back after a while. Don't worry about me. I can take care of myself." He hesitated and smiled. "No good luck days or bad luck days live in the city. Here, all the days are just days."

The patrón had taken more than his money. He had stolen his spirit.

He stopped at the door. "It doesn't matter when the rains come, because here the water is inside the walls. It doesn't matter if the moon is full or new, because all the streets have lights. And it doesn't matter which way the wind blows, because it has to follow the streets just like the rest of us."

I knew he spoke the truth. But I longed for the way things used to be in my village, where each day was a god, each season was a god, and each direction was a god. And we, the people of the center, lived in the middle of every one of them and they lived all around us. We breathed them and they breathed us and we lived them and they lived us. We depended on each other. Nobody was ever alone, not them, not us. But he was right: that world didn't exist here.

My fears slipped beneath the surface when Martín returned later with money in his pocket. Nothing bad had happened to him. Maybe he was right. Maybe in the city the gods of the five unlucky days got caught up in the rush of days and they lost their identity and became nameless days the way we became nameless people. Maybe.

Sunday Martín was himself again, and in the evening we sat facing each other in the semi-darkness of our empty building, sharing secrets.

"What reminds you of home?" he asked.

Talk of home made me uncomfortable, but it seemed to be important to him, so I didn't say anything. Instead I reached for the white plastic bag I carried with me everywhere. The only things from home were my hair ribbons and a picture of the Virgin. I laid them on the floor between us.

"Do they mean a lot to you?"

I thought for a moment. "Not anymore."

"Mine do." Silence sat between us. Martín got up on his knees and reached into his pocket. "This was my father's." He laid a piece of knife handle on the floor. It was carved out of a green stone.

I picked it up and turned it over in my hands. "It's very pretty."

He reached back into the pocket. "Jade is the color of the gods' hearts."

I dropped the knife handle as if it had suddenly become sharp.

Next to it Martín placed a small clay figure. "I found this in my father's cornfield. He gave it to me for luck." He looked up at me sheepishly. "It's the sun god." He reached into his pocket one more time and pulled out a bottlecap. "My little sister gave me this for luck." He looked up at me with a smile. "With so much luck, how could I not survive?"

I smiled back. "Of course. You're much too strong to fail."

"They were strong. Until the day the army came. I was the only one who got away. I had all their luck."

He wiped his eye with the back of his hand. Then he picked up the figure of the sun god, the bottlecap and the jade knife handle and slipped them one by one into his pocket as if they were his family. I put my ribbon and the picture of the Virgin back into my plastic bag. At least I still had a village. He had nothing.

Flor began to whimper faint little cries. I took her out of my rebozo and laid her on my lap. "Wet and hungry again, aren't you?"

She doubled her little hands into tiny fists and yelled hungrily. Her mouth searched for something to suck. I unwound the wet cloth and wrapped a clean one around her. Her bottom was full of sores. She didn't pee very often, but when she did it was always a dark yellow. Maybe that's why she had sores. She found her fist and sucked it noisily. I picked her up, lifted my blouse and put her to my breast.

Martín leaned against the wall and watched us, one leg doubled in front of him. "You're a good mother."

I looked up and smiled. "Thank you."

"Is your name really Rosa?" he asked. "Like the flower?"

I nodded. "My mother said I was a gift from La Virgen."

His eyes lit up. "Really? Then you must be very special."

I lowered my eyes and shook my head slightly. I fingered my rebozo. I didn't want to be special. That made everything worse. It was better to be no one. He didn't seem to notice the discomfort his words had brought me.

He toyed with his shoelaces for a moment and then looked up at me. "Has anyone ever given you a rose?"

"No."

His face lit up. "Then I shall bring you one!"

The idea brought a smile to my face. "A rose, for me? Where will you get a rose?"

"You don't need to wonder about that part. Leave it to me."

"What color will it be?"

Martín looked surprised. "What color do you want?"

I thought for a moment. What color should it be? "White."

"Why white? Why not red?"

Red. The word made my stomach queasy. Not red. Red was the color the patrón always gave the señora. The trashcan bled with red roses at that house. No. No red. White. It had to be white. White was the opposite of red. It was as far away from red as possible. It was the Virgin's color. "I've never seen a white rose," I said.

Martín stood up and bowed an exaggerated bow before me. "Then a white rose it is, for your majesty."

I giggled. Your majesty. My insides felt soft and warm. "I've never had a rose of my very own before." I twirled a lock of my hair. "But I've smelled them. They are sweet."

His gaze met mine. "What will you do with your rose?"

I thought for a moment. "First I'll hold it by the stem and take off the thorns."

He nodded. "I forgot about that part."

"And then I'll look at it from the top to the bottom. I'll say 'Rose, you are so beautiful.'"

Martín laughed. "You're going to talk to a rose?"

I nodded. "Of course. It's my rose. I can talk to it if I want to."

"Okay. And then what?"

"Then I will notice how the leaves connect to the stem and how the blossom sits on the very top." I held an invisible white rose in my hand and examined it with my fingers. "And then, after I know everything about my rose, I will hold it to my nose and inhale its sweet nature." I held my white rose to my nostrils and took a deep breath. "Mmmm, I'll remember this forever." I looked up at him. "That's what I'm going to do with my rose."

"And when it wilts?"

"I shall pluck the petals and put them in my rebozo so my baby will sleep in their sweetness. And we will both dream Our Lady is holding us in her arms." I looked at him and smiled. "It will be the most wonderful time."

That night we played pretend until our fingers burned from the cold.

"Tomorrow I bring you a white rose." Martín's voice floated softly across the empty concrete floor, closing my eyelids with its promises and leaving a smile on my face.

Sleep led me through fields of sweet-smelling white roses. As we wafted through the night, buttons, scattered about the floor, wept for what they had become and begged to be white rose petals once more.

The next day I sat by the supermarket and held out my hand, but no number of coins looked as pretty to me as the rose I was to have that evening. Later, as orange, red and turquoise painted the western sky, I walked back to our big house. I watched my own feet plod along on the sidewalk and smiled, thinking about the rose that was coming to me.

The beans that night tasted of roses, the tortillas felt as soft as rose petals, the sidewalk home was strewn with trash that, if given a choice, might have been rose petals. The whole world had become a rose. A rose with the scent of the fields, the warmth of the sun and the softness of my mother's touch. My rose would take me home again, if only for a little while.

Martín wasn't at the big house when I arrived, so Flor and I waited in the darkness. "It's lonesome with no one to talk to," I confided. "Except you, of course."

Flor made soft gurgling sounds. Her eyes were soft and round and her little mouth was so perfectly formed it was difficult to believe it was real. I ran my fingers over her lips and a warm feeling filled my chest.

"I wish you were older. Then we could play games."

She blinked. I thought it was her way of saying she would someday. I heard footsteps outside. They stopped. I sat up, alert for what might come next. I whispered, "Martín, is that you?"

No answer but silence. I leaned back against the wall and closed my eyes. The floor was harder without Martín, the walls colder. I slept fitfully, waking at every noise.

He wasn't there in the morning, either. There was no sign of him. No candle, no rose, no paper from the tortillas he had eaten. Just half-empty concrete bags and empty soda cans from some other time.

I nursed Flor and changed her and then went to the market for a cup of hot milk and a roll. I ate and then hurried to my place in front of the supermarket. Something must have delayed him. He'd be there tonight when we arrived. He promised.

I thought of my rose all day long. That day I didn't get enough money for beans, but I did have enough to buy tortillas. But it didn't matter, because tonight I would have a rose of my very own.

Flor cried little whimpering cries all day. I held her close to me and nursed her even though my breasts felt empty. It was cloudy. Maybe she was cold; maybe she was hungry. I don't know. I hoped she wasn't sick. She didn't seem to be much bigger now than when she was born, nearly three months ago.

One of the boys who washed cars in the street shared water with me. He was working there when I arrived and knew all the secrets of the supermarket and where the best trash was dumped in the vacant lot behind it. "I brought you some water." He set the bucket down beside me. "Do you want me to take care of Flor while you wash her clothes?"

He couldn't have been more than six, but he washed cars every day and took home enough money for his mother and two little brothers. I wished I could be like him. I got up from the sidewalk and gave Flor to him. "Be very careful."

He nodded. "I take care of her like she was my own sister, you know that."

I tousled his hair. "You don't have a sister, silly." I picked up the bucket and headed toward the vacant lot behind the supermarket.

"I might!" he called.

"I'll be right back," I called over my shoulder. "Hold her close. Keep her warm." I walked past the supermarket and through a hole in the fence that surrounded the empty lot, swinging the bucket. For a brief moment Micaela and I were fetching water from the river again, laughing and giggling and trying not to spill too much of it. My village perched above us and all the faces smiled. I was home, where I belonged.

Home. I could never go back home. The empty lot was not home. It was not beautiful. It was not a part of the earth that anyone respected. It was where people threw things they had used up—like us. I scrounged through the mounds of trash until I found enough detergent to wash the baby's clothes. I think it made them too stiff, because she always had sores. I had seen mothers in my village clean their babies, but I had nothing to clean my baby with. I promised her when she got older she would not have to wear the cloths anymore.

I poured the detergent into the bucket and began to scrub. Children in my village didn't wear pants, and they could pee when and where they wanted to, but this was the city and things were different here. People didn't like babies without pants. Like something about it was wrong. There was no water to rinse the cloths with so I draped them on the fence to dry, poured the dirty water onto the grass and returned to my place in front of the supermarket. The boy was singing to Flor when I returned. She was making gurgling noises. If I had had a brother, I would have chosen him.

There was no rose that night or the next or the one after that. Something must have happened. Martín could take care of himself. He'd probably had to work late. Maybe the patrón let him sleep in the store. Maybe the patrón had taken him off into the countryside to work on another project. He'd tell me when I saw him.

The nights were long and cold and lonely. I tried pretending the king was away on a long trip and that he would come back with a treasure, but it was no fun pretending all by myself. Martín had become part of our lives, and without him they were empty.

One morning I didn't go to my place by the supermarket. I knew I would be hungry later, but I had to find Martín. After I nursed and changed Flor, I studied the signs on the corners and sounded out the letters until I found the street where he worked. I walked along the street, looking into each store until I found the hardware store where he worked.

The man behind the counter glanced up. He was a mestizo and much taller than I. A large apron covered the middle of his belly.

"I'm looking for Martín," I said.

"Who?'

"The boy who works here."

He shook his head. "He's not here." He rearranged some things beneath the glass countertop, avoiding my eyes. "Anything else?"

"Do you know where he is?" I stood on the other side of the counter, careful not to touch. I had seen the police called when an Indian had done nothing more than touch.

"Yes." There was an odd tone in his voice. He turned his back to me and began to rearrange cans of paint.

I waited. He turned each can so that the labels all faced front. I was beginning to think he had forgotten me when he finally spoke.

"They shot him." He reached on the shelf for a can of paint and turned it around to face the front. "They told him to stop, but he didn't."

The pain in my chest stopped my breath as surely as if he had plunged a knife into my heart. "No! It can't be!"

He turned, positioned both hands on the counter and straightened out his arms. "That's the way it goes," he said with a shrug.

The earth gave way beneath me. The jaws of the Earth Monster sprang open and clasped my feet. It bound my arms, squeezed my chest, pulled me into a suffocating mix of garlic and stale cigarettes. I staggered out onto the sidewalk.

Chapter Fifteen

The next morning I awoke and stepped outside onto the sidewalk and into the rays of the spring sun. Two years ago my grandmother had died. Now it was my turn. It felt right. Like I had reached the end of a big circle. Rays of sunlight penetrated my body, making my blood tingle. Odd that the fullness of life should come now, at the end.

I stood up and shook the dust off, straightened my clothes and ran my fingers through my hair. It no longer mattered that my face was dirty, that my baby smelled bad, that my hair was matted or the nights we had both been hungry and cold. That was all over now. I felt free now.

I felt in my pocket and pulled out a coin. It would be enough left for a roll or for a cup of hot milk. Which was it to be? I savored the taste of each on my tongue and decided on the milk. By the time we reached the stand at the market, I had drunk that cup of milk many times.

I gave the woman at the counter the coin, took the cup and sat down at a table as far from her as I could find. Today she wasn't going to tell me to leave. Today I was going to stay as long as I wanted, until I had drunk every drop from the cup. I held the warm liquid to my lips and took a deep breath. The mountains lived in that cup. I took a sip and then another. I could taste the grasses and feel the sun. It was a fine day to be going to the spirit world and I was going to savor every minute of it.

I touched the front of my blue blouse with my fingertips. The same sky, that infinite blue sky, was in the milk. I lifted the cup to my lips and swallowed. Flowers. Dark earth. They were both there. Tingling with life. I held the cup in my hands and let its warmth fill my fingers. The whole world was in that cup. I smiled. The whole world had come to say goodbye and hello to me today.

When I was little the days began like today—full of magic and beauty. They were delicious when the sun baked the earth dry, and when the rains persuaded the hard earth to become mud instead; when the sky decorated the nighttime with stars and when it poured beautiful colors down onto our village; when the seeds we had planted woke up and the hills dressed in blossoms. That's how it would be in the spirit world, too. I was sure of it. I got up and returned the empty cup to the woman on the other side of the counter. I looked straight into her eyes. "Thank you."

I walked around the market. Someone there had to know of a place. I stopped in front of a woman who arranged a table piled high with shiny green chili peppers, tangy oranges, and white bulbs of garlic bursting out of their papery skins.

"Can you tell me if there is a place to leave babies who have no parents?"

She shook her head and pointed to the woman across from her. "She can tell you."

I turned around. A plump woman my mother's age hung up garlands of dried chili peppers the color of blood. "At the mission." She looked at me. "Doesn't that baby have a mother?"

I smiled. "Not for long." It felt good to say it. "Where is the mission?"

She gave me a look of disbelief, but pointed behind her toward the hills on the north side of the city. "On the outskirts. Where the road starts to climb."

I walked toward the mountains in the direction she pointed. Several times I stopped to ask a passerby. I was on the right road, just impatient to get there.

Finally a woman pointed to a large wooden door on the opposite side of the street. "You're standing in front of it," she said.

I looked at the house she pointed to. Not only was there a mission, but also it was on a busy road, just after a curve. It was perfect. "Saint

John the Baptist, you have been kind to me!" I said. "You will meet me, won't you?"

I crossed the street and rang the bell that hung outside the mission door. I waited, eyeing the trucks that barreled past. Yes, it was perfect. Quick, easy, painless. What more could I ask for? A woman opened the door. She had dark, curly hair and pale skin. Her eyes were a deep blue. They reminded me of something, but I didn't want to remember what it was. It was too late for memories. I shoved them aside.

She smiled at me. "Come in."

Instead I opened my rebozo and showed her my baby. "I have only come to leave the baby," I said.

She stepped outside and looked inside my rebozo, but didn't reach for her. "Is she yours?"

I nodded.

"She's beautiful. Why do you want to leave her?" She took a step forward and ran her fingers down the side of my baby's face. She spoke Spanish with an accent. So did I, but hers was different.

I pulled the rebozo back and looked up at her. "I'm going to the Otherworld."

"Oh."

I thought she understood what I meant, even though she tilted her head to one side as if she had a question. I took Flor out of the rebozo and placed her in the woman's arms. Flor whimpered.

The woman held her but didn't move. "Why don't you come in and tell me about it?" Her eyes locked onto mine, but her voice was soft. I could feel the insistence of her gaze and I struggled to break away from it.

I shook my head and took a step back. "No, I can't." I turned halfway around as a bus raced down the hill and skidded on the dirt road. I turned back to her and shouted through the swirling dust. "I have to go now."

She nodded and looked into my eyes, but she stood firm. "When are you coming back for her?" Her gaze was too strong for me. I couldn't give up now. Freedom was too close.

Her eyes knew too much. I looked instead at the concrete beneath my feet and shook my head. I had made my decision and it felt good. I was not going back. Not even for this. Flor's weak whimpers grew louder.

"What's her name?" Her voice was persistent. Stronger than I wanted.

"She doesn't have a name," I lied, not daring to look at her.

"Then what shall we call her?"

Why did she care? Didn't she know who we were? Didn't she know we were disposable people? The ones who didn't matter? I shook my head. "Whatever you want."

She stood firm. "I can't accept her without a name." She held her out to me.

This was taking too much time. It was becoming complicated. I shifted from one foot to the other. "You can call her Flor." There. She had what she wanted. Now I was done with it.

I turned to walk away, but the woman reached out and put her hand on my shoulder. Her touch reminded me of my grandmother's. I stopped and let the warmth of her fingers sink into me. Odd that something as simple as a touch could stir up so many feelings. I craved the touch of another human being and at the same time recoiled from the idea, drowning in waves of repulsion. I wouldn't feel anything when they picked my body up off the road. Or when they put it in the earth. Maybe this was the last time I would feel anything ever—except for the truck. One big jolt and then nothing. I stood there, aware of her hand on my shoulder.

"What's your name?"

Ties again. She was binding us to her. It wasn't what I had come for. I had come to cut ties. I couldn't move. I fought with myself, wanting to be loosened forever and longing to feel her touch in the same forever. "Rosa."

"Rosa." She repeated my name slowly. Her hand moved down from my shoulder to my elbow.

The touch of her hand weakened my resolve. The sound of her voice stilled my feet. The pull of her eyes made me waver in my desire. She took my arm and drew me slowly toward her. "Come inside, Rosa. Let's talk."

Her eyes pulled me in and held me, against my will. He had pulled me like that. Against my will, he had touched me. Her touch was not like his. It was soft and kind. But just as dangerous. I broke loose from her grasp and shook my head. "I have to go. They're waiting for me." I stepped toward the road, then stopped. The determination I had felt earlier was fast waning. The thought frightened me. Determination was all I had left.

"Who's waiting for you?" Her voice called me back again and I turned around. Her arms swaddled Flor as if they had held many babies.

I looked into her eyes. "Saint John the Baptist, my grandmother and the gods."

She nodded. "I understand." She looked at my baby and then at me again. "Do you want to feed her before you go?" She held her out to me. "So she will remember you."

I hesitated. I thought I would be in the Otherworld by now. I would give my baby away and walk into a truck and it would all be over. It wasn't as easy as I envisioned. I shook my head. "No. I hardly have milk." I turned to walk away. "It's better here." She was saying too many things. I had made a decision and it had given me strength. Now that strength was dissolving. I had to leave now, before it was totally gone.

"Rosa."

Her voice trailed after me, wrapping itself around me, making me want to stop. I fought against it and kept walking toward the street.

"I know your village. Shall I take Flor to your people?" Her words surrounded me with promises of possibility.

I stopped and turned back, then willed myself to turn away. I had to do it now, while I still could. I had lost faith in possibility. "I don't have a village."

Her voice followed me, insistent. "Your skirt says you do. Your blouse says you do."

"No, that was before. I don't belong anywhere now." I could hear the roar of a motor. It sounded like a truck. It was the one I was waiting for. I closed my eyes and stepped into the street.

I opened my arms to death. To the promises of death. To the certainty of death. The lure of sweet nothingness beckoned, enticed, persuaded. Yes, oh yes! To be no longer, to feel no more. To tumble into oblivion. To not be and to never have been—oh yes! A thousand times yes!

Chapter Sixteen

Someone screamed. It couldn't have been me. If I had made any noise at all, I would have laughed. I would have opened my mouth wider than ever in my life and laughed a big, joyful belly laugh. I wouldn't have screamed.

Brakes screeched, dust swirled, and my body hit the pavement. A jolt, and then rolling in a cloud of dust. Someone rolled with me. My grandmother had come for me, come to roll me into the Otherworld. It was easier than I had imagined. I felt no pain.

When the rolling stopped, I opened my eyes. An unexpected weight lay heavy on my chest. Through the churning spirals of dust, I saw, not the face of my grandmother, but instead the face of a man. Eyes widened by fear, forehead dripping with sweat, his face hidden behind a mask of dust. His body lay powerfully against mine, pressing it into jagged bits of gravel, holding it prisoner in the pain of this world. I had rolled, not into the future, but backward, into the hell of the past. I looked into his face and then everything went black.

I woke as the afternoon light was beginning to turn the color of blood oranges. My body lay sunken into the narrow cot. Dust covered my face and arms like a shroud. The acrid smells of burning oil and grit coated my nostrils. A soft pillow held my head; clean sheets seduced my body with false promises.

I forced my eyes to open. A chair, a table and an armoire with a mirror on the front. The door to the Otherworld had slammed shut in my face. I had escaped nothing. I was disposable, even to the gods.

A knock on the door interrupted. The door opened. "Rosa, how do you feel?"

It was the voice of the woman I had given my baby to. The woman I had trusted. I turned my head toward the wall and tried to shut out her voice.

The springs of the narrow bed squeaked as she sat down. Squeaked like when the patrón lay on top of me.

"Would you like something to eat? We have soup."

Spasms grabbed my stomach. I shook my head, clenched my jaws to hold back the tears and buried my face in my hands. She had betrayed me. I had asked her to keep my baby and let me go and now she had us both. The patrón had betrayed me. He was supposed to give me work, not hurt me. My father had betrayed me. I was his child, not an animal to be sold in the market. "Please go away," I whispered.

She got up and moved toward the door. "Your baby is crying for you." She waited. "I thought you might like to know. We've given her a bottle."

The springs squeaked again when she got up. Footsteps faded into the distance and the door closed. The patrón had left and another Sunday was over. I pulled the blanket around me and tumbled into darkness.

Soft purple bathed the morning when the woman returned. Birds chirped outside the window and a soft breeze played with the thin curtains. The smells of hot chocolate and fresh bread sneaked in through the open doorway like curious children.

The woman stood just inside the door. "Rosa," she said. "Your baby needs you. You'll have to get up and take care of her."

The smells of life. How they teased, how they taunted. I turned my face away from her toward the wall. She walked around my bed, took my chin in her hand and made me look at her. She smiled and held out her hand. "Come on, we're eating breakfast. You must get up."

I shut my eyes and covered my face with my hands. The gods had not protected me when I wanted to live, now they refused to let me die. I was trapped in the in-between world. Of what use was I to them? Didn't they know my kind was not worth it?

"I'll give you a minute," she said softly. She stood up, walked out and the door closed behind her.

A girl came in later. I barely glanced at her. "I'm taking care of your baby."

She waited for a reply, but I didn't give one.

Her voice was insistent. "She's hungry. Señora Sara says you need to get up and feed her."

But her words could not lure me out. Instead I buried myself more deeply into the blanket and gave myself back to the Nothingness I had summoned. I could feel it pulling me closer. It reached out and wrapped itself around me and I felt myself slowly dissolve. No time, no space, no life, no death—just nothingness. I felt as invisible as the air, as free as the wind, as light as the clouds. The morning melted into afternoon, then drifted into night and I drifted with it.

With the morning the light in my head became brighter, the darkness of the void more seductive. The woman came into my room and sat down on the edge of my bed. The squeak of the springs brought the patrón with her. I covered my face with my arms, steeling myself against the stench of garlic and cigarettes and dreading what came with them. Her voice cut through my nightmare and brought its own. "Rosa, you're going to have to leave the mission."

Her words stung. She got up and walked toward the door. "I want you to leave now. You'll have to take your baby with you."

I forced myself to open my eyes. I tried to speak. My mouth was dry and it was difficult to get the words out. "Señora, I'll go, but please keep her. I beg you."

The woman stood in the doorway and rested one hand on the frame. "We don't keep babies unless their mothers stay with them. If you want to die, that's your business, but this house is a place for the living. You and your baby will have to do your dying somewhere else." She started to shut the door. "I'll go get her."

Her words left a dull ache in my chest. I sat up and looked around. The room tilted crazily before me. The face in the mirror shocked me. Hollow eyes, dirty face, uncombed hair. I touched her cheek. Was this me?

A moment later the door opened again and the woman returned.

My baby was whimpering. The woman put her in my arms, stood back and crossed her arms across her chest. "Come on, I'll show you the way out."

I held Flor with one arm and wiped my face with my sleeve while I swung my legs onto the floor. This wasn't what I wanted. Not like this. Things were going wrong and I didn't know how to stop them. I looked around for my shoes, but they weren't there. I looked up at her. "I don't know where my shoes are."

She held out her hand. "It doesn't matter. The dead don't wear shoes."

I swallowed hard. She extended her hand and pulled me up. I faltered, weak and afraid. I looked down into my baby's eyes. I couldn't take her with me and I couldn't leave her there. What was I to do? Her face was clean and her hair had been brushed. Her whimpering turned to soft cooing noises. She smelled freshly bathed and someone had pinned a tiny ribbon in her hair. But it was her eyes that caught me. I sucked in my breath. "Señora, I think she knows me!"

The woman smiled. "She's not crying anymore. She knows you are her mother."

Her words surprised me. "She knows that?"

"Yes. You are the whole world to her."

The whole world! I was that important? I stared at her, not daring to believe it.

An invisible hand pushed us out of the room, and before I had a chance to reconsider we had reached the heavy wooden door that opened onto the street.

The woman with the accent was caressing my baby's cheek. "Goodbye dear, and God bless." She rested her hand lightly on my shoulder, then opened the door.

The noise of life filled my ears. I couldn't think. Outside trucks raced by, dust swirled, people hurried to get somewhere, honked horns, carried bundles and problems with equal fervor. The machinery of living engulfed me. All of a sudden I was no longer convinced I was doing the right thing.

"Señora," I began. "Does she really know who I am?"

The woman with the accent nodded. "Yes." I heard the same kindness in her voice that I had felt in her touch. She pushed us through the door, and then shut it firmly, leaving us alone on the doorstep.

I faced the street. In front of me, trucks promising a quick solution roared by, leaving clouds of dust and noise. Behind me and behind the wooden door lay life and uncertainty. And in between them lay a tiny person who thought I was the most important person in the whole world. I reached down and she grasped one finger. "How can I leave you behind?" I asked, choking on my question. "But what kind of life can you have here, with no family to love you, no Ancestors to guide you, with no village to show you who you are? No grandmother to show you beauty, no father to—."

Suddenly I stood next to my father on the village square. I was three again. I held onto his hand and buried my face in his pants leg as horses thundered past. I felt the earth tremble as their hooves pounded and I felt his hand reassure me that I was safe. The earth trembled under my feet again. I looked up. This time it was my baby who grasped my hand.

A sweet sensation on my tongue and I knew myself as the flower of the sacred Ceiba and the blade of grass. Crisp air rushed into my lungs and I became the mountain that nestled against the sky. I stood on the dark, damp earth and drank its cool waters from the deep wells of my people. The leaves of dried cornstalks rustled in my ears. The smells of freshly turned dirt, our sheep and tortillas cooking on the comal enveloped me. The peculiar sound of leather sandals slapping against cobblestones, the reassuring clicking of the hooves of our sheep—the circle continued and we were part of it. I turned away from the street and knocked on the door.

Chapter Seventeen

The señora showed us into a room with a long table where other girls sat dipping fragrant slices of bread into hot milk. "This is Rosa," she said. "And Flor."

I blushed and lowered my head. I braced against the looks that would tell me to keep away, but there weren't any. One by one shy voices repeated my name.

The woman took Flor from me and motioned for me to sit at the table. "Eat some breakfast. We have a lot of work to do today." Then she left the room.

Someone placed a gourd of warm milk in front of me. Without lifting my head I glanced around the table to see what the other girls were doing. Silently they broke off pieces of bread and dipped them into the warm milk. I dipped my bread into the bowl in front of me, not daring to look up. As they finished, some got up and took their bowls into the kitchen. Others just sat.

I had just drunk the last of the milk when the woman came back. "You'd better bathe first." She handed me a neatly folded pile of clothes. "You can wear these while your own clothes dry." She spoke to one of the girls seated at the far end of the table. "Micaela, will you take Rosa to the showers?"

My breath stopped. Micaela? I looked up. Surely it wasn't my Micaela.

The girl got up from the far end of the table and limped slowly toward me. She lifted her face as she reached my side. I gasped. "Micaela! It is you."

"Yes," came the monotone reply.

I stood up and reached out to her. Once I would have thrown my arms around her without a second thought. Now I felt awkward, as if I had mistaken her for someone else.

Her eyes stared vacantly past me as if her body were nothing more than a hollow shell. I drew back, horrified. I touched my own face. Did I look like that, too? Were we no more than empty remnants of people who had once lived? And yet my baby knew who I was… Instinctively I reached out and took the hand of the girl who had once been my best friend. It rested lifelessly in mine. "Show me where the showers are."

Micaela walked with a limp. I didn't remember that. We reached the bathroom and she stopped.

"Why are you here?" I asked.

"I worked for a family. You know what happens." There was no strength in her voice, no lilt, no laughter. Everything that once defined her was absent. She turned away from me and gestured to the shower. "Go in."

I walked into the large stall.

Behind me she reached up and pulled a plastic curtain across the opening. "I'll sit and wait on the bench."

I leaned against the shower wall and put my hand over my stomach. Micaela.

What terrible thing had happened to her? I doubled my hand and pounded my fist against the wall. I grabbed all the patrones in Santa María by the neck and squeezed the life out of them, watched their ugly veins turn purple and watched them fight for breath and watched their eyes bulge out of their heads and watched them die. Then I spat on them. It wasn't enough. I wanted to do it over and over again. Instead I swallowed, took a deep breath and called from inside the stall. "Micaela, where were the gods?"

She didn't answer.

I choked. "Didn't they care what was happening to us?" I pulled back the shower curtain. Micaela sat, staring with vacant eyes at the wall. I don't even know that she heard my question. I shook my head.

Perhaps it had been a mistake, coming back.

I shut the curtain and withdrew into the confines of the shower. I leaned against the wall. Without warning the tiny stall became another place. Through the haze of what I knew to be sacred smoke, they formed a circle. How many—twenty? Fifty? Men and women. From many tribes, from many mountains. Where do you think we come back from each year at Muertos? Where do we come from and where do we return?

Their simple questions jolted me. I didn't know the answer. I had never considered it. One by one they approached me, looked into my eyes, blew sacred smoke onto my forehead, touched their fingers to the center of my chest.

"I don't know," I whispered.

No place. There is no place else.

"No!" I cried. "That can't be!" But I knew they spoke the truth. There was no place to disappear into...there was only me...and Me...and Infinite Me...everywhere and for all time...

I slumped down onto the floor and buried my head between my knees.

A thin voice pushed through the plastic curtain. "Rosa?"

I pulled myself off the floor. Life reached beyond death. There was no end to it.

Old faces wrinkled with a thousand years of living looked into mine, all whispering the same thing: Everything springs into being out of this moment. You are the center.

"Rosa?"

The idea stunned my soul, left my mind reeling and stormed the door to my heart.

Micaela called again. "Do you know how to turn on the water?"

I took a deep breath. "Then that changes everything," I whispered. I opened the plastic curtain, stepped outside and put my arms around my best friend.

She tolerated my embrace as if it were an ordeal and I a stranger. When she pulled away I stepped back inside the shower stall and closed the curtain, took off my clothes and opened the faucet.

Much later I opened the curtain and stepped out. Micaela sat huddled on the little bench, still staring vacantly at the wall. "Now you go to wash your clothes."

I took her hand in mine. "Was it bad for you?"

She shrugged and withdrew her hand.

"I'm sorry." I searched her eyes for the spark that I knew so well. "Micaela, come back. I need us to be who we used to be."

She tilted her head as though she recognized me. Her voice was hesitant and faint.

"We carried water."

I nodded. "We used to do everything together."

"Oh."

Her eyes flickered with recognition, then lapsed back into a vacant stare. She had come out for a moment, but then I lost her again. I knew well the place she hid: I had spent much time there myself.

She got up from the bench and shuffled toward the staircase. I followed her up the spiral stairs to the washboards. On the roof I washed my clothes and hung them up to dry.

Micaela stood in the middle of the clotheslines, stretched her arms out and turned around slowly with a faint smile on her face. She pointed to a distant mountain. "There, beyond the mountain." She looked at me, as if waiting for confirmation.

"Yes, you remember." I walked over to the edge of the roof and peered over the side. I stayed there a long time, thinking. It felt good to be above the street. A good place to think. When I turned around she was staring at me.

"It's not high enough. You'll only break your legs."

I knew then there was no place here for secrets.

"Rosa, your baby needs a bath." The voice of the señora spiraled up the staircase, wound around the laundry and found me among the clotheslines.

Micaela tugged on my sleeve. "We have to go down now."

I nodded and took her hand. We walked down to the foot of the spiral staircase where the señora waited.

"I don't think I've told you my name," she said, holding out her hand. "It's Sara."

I bowed slightly, but she didn't retrieve her hand. Instead she reached out for mine and shook it. "Nobody bows to anybody here," she said. "We're equals."

I was embarrassed for her. She wasn't from here, was she? She must not know we were Indians. She had white skin and we had dark skin—how could she not know? Everyone else did. She would find out soon enough and then we would all bow.

She led me along the hallway and stopped in front of a door painted bright pink. "Your baby is in here, waiting for you to bathe her." Her fingers briefly touched the fabric of my sleeve and then she was gone. I stared after her and then at the closed door. When did life get like this? Overwhelming, demanding, intense. I turned the door handle and walked into the room.

A girl I had seen at breakfast looked up from a pile of clean clothes and smiled. "Coming to bathe your baby?"

I nodded. Flor lay awake in a pale green hammock that was strung across the far corner of the room.

The girl got up from the table with the mound of clothes and walked across to a little sink, reached underneath it and pulled out a small plastic tub. "Here, you can use this," she said, holding it out to me.

I stood in the doorway, not moving.

She smiled. "Come in and close the door. You don't want a draft, do you? She'll catch a chill."

I shook my head and did as she instructed. "No."

She reached into a small cabinet and pulled out a sponge, a bar of soap and a towel, and handed them to me. "Here."

I took them but when I didn't move, she giggled. "Well don't just stand there." She moved a pile of folded clothes from a second table. "You can fill the tub and put it here. That way you have room to dry and dress her." She went back to sorting clothes. Her hands sorted and folded as if they had always known what to do, which pieces to pick now and which to leave for later. They moved quickly, choosing, smoothing, folding, then smoothing again and finally leaving it in a neat pile. Her movements were logical and sure.

I bowed my head, trying to hide my shyness and not knowing what to do with my feelings of helplessness. One hand held the tub, the other the soap and sponge. The towel was draped over my arm. I put everything down on the table where she had said to and looked across the room at Flor. I didn't know how to bathe a baby, not even mine. I remembered the first month at Angelina's house, how she and the upstairs maid had taken turns bathing her and how I had busied myself doing other things, too afraid to even watch. After that there had been no place to bathe her, except for the empty lot by the supermarket and it was much too cold for that.

The girl sat down and began turning a shirt right side out. "You might want to put the water in the tub before you pick her up," she said. She smoothed the shirt and then folded it neatly.

I nodded self-consciously. Was she watching me? Did she know what I was thinking? "Of course." I picked up the tub and went to the sink, turned the faucet and filled the tub with water.

"Make sure it's not too hot or too cold," the girl called.

My knees felt weak. Of course, how stupid I was. I had filled the tub with cold water. Flor would get sick. I poured the water out and let it run until it was hot. Hot water would burn her. I poured it out as well, stopped and took a breath. I could do this. It was only about putting a tiny person in a small bit of water. That was all.

I turned both faucets, adjusting the water until it was warm, but not hot, then filled the tub and carried it to the little table. I wanted to look like I knew what I was doing. I wanted her to think I knew as much about babies as she did.

I picked Flor up out of the hammock and carried her over to the tub. "Do I take off her clothes?"

The girl was at my side in an instant. "Yes, of course."

I turned red. "Of course, I knew that," I stammered. "I'm so nervous, I just forgot."

Flor began to cry.

The girl put her hand on my shoulder. "It's okay. Don't worry about it. It happens all the time. Do you want me to bathe her today?" she hesitated. "Until you get used to the way we do things around here?"

The idea of bathing a baby was daunting. A million things could go wrong. I looked at Flor, her faint cries escalating into screams. She could slip from my grasp, swallow water and drown. Soap could burn her eyes and make her blind. Water too hot would burn; too cold would make her sick. If she stayed wet too long she could catch a cold and die. Maybe the water itself was not good. I cleared my throat. "Yes, that would be nice."

The girl reached out and took Flor from me. "I can only help you this one time, so stand next to me and watch what I do. You'll have to do it all by yourself next time."

Flor's cries became whimpers.

I watched the girl anxiously, wondering what she thought of a mother who didn't know how to bathe her own child.

She undressed Flor and slid her into the tub. "You do it like this." She held Flor firmly with one hand and dribbled water on her with the other. Flor cried again.

"Is it too hot?" I asked anxiously.

The girl dipped her elbow into the water. "No." She turned her over and showed me her bottom. "She has sores. I think the water stings. That's why she cries."

Red sores covered her bottom. Some were tiny red pinpoints; others were large and watery. I shrank back, embarrassed again at my ignorance and lack of skills.

In the water Flor squirmed and made little crying noises. Maybe this bath wasn't such a good idea. The girl soaped her face and body with a sponge and then rinsed her off with clean water.

I watched carefully. "Will she die from being wet?"

The girl shook her head. "No, I don't think so." She lifted her out of the water with both hands and laid her on a towel to dry her off. "This is what you have to be careful of." She opened a tube of ointment and rubbed it on Flor's bottom. I waited for her to tell me how I knew nothing and how unfit I was to be this child's mother and how I had done everything wrong, but all she did was to tell me to put some on each time I changed her.

I nodded. "I think she'll get better now."

She nodded, sat Flor up, reached for a tiny hairbrush and began to comb her hair back from her face. "She's so pretty. By the way, I don't think you know my name, do you?"

I looked at her, puzzled. Was I supposed to know her name? Was this another of my shortcomings? "No," I faltered. "I'm sorry."

She extended her free hand the way the señora Sara had done. I reached out and shook it.

"I'm Marisol. And you're Rosa. I remember you from breakfast." Marisol put her fingers around Flor's thigh. "See how thin her legs are? They need to be this fat." She made a wide circle with her fingers. "Don't worry, they will be soon." She finished brushing Flor's hair and pinned a tiny pink ribbon on the side of her head. "There now, you're all done. And such a pretty girl!" She picked her up and held her out to me. "Go to your mamá so she can dress you." Glancing up she asked. "How old is she?"

I reached out to take her and shrugged. "She came in the cold. Right after Christmas."

Marisol nodded. "Then she must be about three months." She looked up at me. "She'll be fine, you'll see."

"How do you know so much about babies?" I asked.

She smiled. "It's my responsibility. Here everyone has a responsibility."

Responsibility. The word took me home again, to the time before, when my responsibilities were six chickens and schoolwork and white flowers for Our Lady. Before my failures had brought dishonor.

We dressed Flor in a clean shirt and a clean cloth that Marisol called a diaper. Angelina had given me some diapers. I didn't know what they were called then. Now I did. Marisol showed me how to pin the diaper on Flor and told me to be careful with the pin. She said to put on a clean one six times a day and that I had to wash her bottom every time I changed her. I was glad to finally be able to take care of her properly.

Marisol said during the day Flor would stay in a big room with other babies and at night she would sleep with me. I counted out six diapers from a shelf in the room. She showed me how to fold them. I folded and refolded them for a long time. I wanted to make sure I did it right. Then I put them carefully in a little stack, making sure the edges were lined up perfectly.

Marisol smiled. "That's the way I do it, too."

I fed Flor and then she fell asleep. It was a good morning. Maybe I had made the right choice. So far everything was good. I watched Marisol take care of the babies. I thought I could learn a lot.

Somewhere a clock chimed. Marisol looked up from her responsibilities. "It's time for class," she said. "We're learning to write letters."

I looked at the babies. The tiniest ones lay in little Moses baskets and the older ones napped on blankets on the floor. Flor slept in the pale green hammock in the corner.

"They're okay. Don't worry. Come on."

I left Flor and we walked across the patio into a sunny room. It had lots of tables and chairs. At the front was a board, just like at the school in our village, only nicer. On the wall were pictures of things. Things I didn't know about. Animals and places I had never seen and strange things. There were also pictures of numbers and letters. I knew about those. I liked school already. I sat between Marisol and Micaela at a table and we waited for the teacher to come in.

The door swung open and a tall man strode in. My body stiffened. It was the man from the street. The one who had rolled under the truck with me, not into the Otherworld, but who had kept me in this world. Heat rushed to my face. Panic grabbed me by the neck. My breath caught in my throat. I coughed, choked, felt my breakfast rise. I was a bird caught in a net, kicking and screaming, trying to get free.

The room turned dark and began to whirl. My body slid to the floor. All the secrets I was hiding spilled out onto the floor with it—the shame I felt for what had happened and for being too scared to run away, the guilt for not having fought back harder, the fear of what lay ahead, my lack of preparation for living and the looks and whispers I would certainly receive from others.

Marisol saved my life that day. Her arms held me, her voice pushed past my screams, her words burned themselves into my memory, her eyes took hold of me and refused to let go. She went into the Underworld and brought me back.

In time I learned everything she had said was true. The teacher was kind. In the days that followed, I learned to like him. He said funny things that made us laugh. He told us stories in Spanish and we taught him songs in our language. He couldn't say the words very well, but he tried, and he laughed even when they came out all wrong.

"There's no shame in doing things wrong, only in not doing them at all," he said.

"You come from a long line of greatness. Never be ashamed of who you are, never forget those who came before you." He told us our ancestors were great mathematicians who used the zero before the Europeans did. He said they knew more planets and more stars, more healing plants and more ways to call the gods than the conquerors had. He told us we should be proud of our ancestors and he showed us pictures of great cities they had built. Great cities like Copán, Palenque, and Tikal.

I learned my lessons, but I learned more than that: I began to remember all the things my grandmother had taught me. I began to remember who I was and to whom I belonged. That was his gift to me. I began to feel proud of my people and proud of myself. It was because of the teacher that I came to understand why the One God had made himself a wife. He needed to see himself through another set of eyes to know who he was.

Chapter Eighteen

*T*he empty concrete building of winter seemed far away now. I didn't think about it often. Because when I did, I thought of Martín, and the memory brought sadness to my heart. He had kept me alive that winter. His presence had made the intense cold more bearable, the nights less dark and the hunger not so sharp. It was difficult to think of him as dead. His spirit was so strong and his dream so clear, it seemed inconceivable that his house would not be built or that his life would not be lived.

The one thing that took my mind off Martín was Flor. She was starting to crawl now, and like Marisol had promised, her legs were filling out and were chubby and brown. I loved putting her on the floor of the babies' room and watching her sway back and forth, as she tried to figure out how to make her body move in the direction she wanted. I loved watching her eyes light up when she spied a toy just out of reach and I loved the determination in her eyes to claim it. Marisol and I cheered her on as she lunged, then fell, then lifted herself up again. Every day she got stronger and every day her progress brought peals of laughter from all of us—including Flor, who seemed to understand that her failures were only steps to success.

Not every moment in the mission was as happy. Some were painful. One afternoon we sat in folding chairs in a circle, feet crossed at the ankles and arms crossed in front of us, feeling out in the open and vulnerable. I wished for a table or a desk to lean on for support, but the señora said we needed to lean on each other instead. It was uncomfortable, sitting like that. Micaela sat on my left side, Marisol on the right.

"Micaela," the señora Sara began, "You haven't said anything in a while. Would you like to talk today?"

Instead of waiting for Micaela to answer I stood up and answered for her. Micaela never said anything. She rarely spoke to anyone, much less to the group. Didn't the señora know that? "She doesn't want to talk today."

A hush filled the room and twenty Indian girls sat, afraid to make a move.

Suddenly the señora was addressing me. Her smile couldn't hide a noticeable edge to her voice. "She can speak for herself, Rosa."

"She will, when it's time." I reached down and clasped her hand. I would protect her, even here. Didn't the señora see how fragile she was? Why was she calling on her?

Twenty pairs of eyes darted back and forth between the señora and me. The room screamed with silence. It was hot, then cold. The palms of my hands perspired. I planted my feet firmly on the tile floor and locked my knees.

The señora's eyes burned into mine. "You can't protect her forever."

"I'm not."

The señora's voice softened and she leaned forward in her chair. "She's among friends here. She doesn't need protecting."

"Yes, she does!" I yelled.

"She doesn't!" The señora shouted. She stood up, sending her chair crashing onto the floor behind her. No one moved. Her voice returned to its normal pitch. "She needs encouraging." The señora looked around the room. "She needs to be encouraged to come out and be who she is. We all do."

I shook my head. "No!" I said. "If someone had protected her, she wouldn't be here. Neither would I." I gestured at the group. "Neither would any of us. None of us would be here now if our parents had taken care of us like they were supposed to."

"Protection isn't everything," the señora said quietly. She lowered her head and spoke to the floor as if recalling painful memories. "It can snuff the life out of you, kill your passions, fill you with self-doubt." Her voice wavered. "Too much protection can strangle your dreams and keep you from ever living your life." She looked up. "Sometimes you have to run a long way and cut yourself off from the people you care about to escape the loving grasp of protection."

I stood firm, held Micaela's hand in mine. Silence echoed off the walls. Minutes passed. No one said anything. Twenty girls stared at crossed ankles and the floor beyond. Then Micaela's hand slipped from mine. The squeak of a chair, followed by the clump of a foot on the tile floor, broke the silence. Twenty Indian girls covered their mouths and held their breaths.

Micaela stood up. A flicker of understanding brushed across her face. The corners of her mouth turned up in a slight smile. "I remember this." She stopped, looked at the faces in the circle. "We're a family, aren't we?"

I looked across the circle. The señora looked back at me.

Micaela limped across the circle and left the room. The other girls quickly followed. The señora and I remained, face to face.

"I'm sorry I yelled," I said, bowing my head.

She turned to pick up her chair. In a hushed tone she said, "Nobody bows to anybody here. We're all equal."

I lifted my head. "That's love, isn't it?"

Flor was no longer content with crawling and was now beginning to pull herself up on her bowed little legs. Her feet seemed to touch the floor tentatively, unsure of the new sensation. They arched themselves into an impossible stance and her body swayed back and forth, hanging on fiercely to whatever was at hand.

Day after day Sara and Marisol and I watched as she tottered between the desire to walk on her own and wanting the safety of a firm hand.

"She's like you, isn't she?" Sara said one day.

I blushed and turned my head away.

Sara patted my shoulder. "It's okay. We all learn to walk in our own time."

In many ways Flor was like me. We both longed for the freedom to roam, but she was still innocent of the dangers of the world and I lived in dread of the day freedom would make me confront those dangers.

Freedom approached cautiously, in tiny footsteps. After having nightmares about Flor drowning in the bath water, I finally became comfortable with the idea of bathing her. It was never her concern: on the contrary, Flor enjoyed it. She laughed and splashed and kicked the whole time, often leaving me as wet as she was. In the beginning I was uncomfortable with how intimate this ritual of touching was, even with a baby, but I gradually got used to it and eventually came to enjoy it almost as much as Flor.

For the most part the mission was safe and predictable. I knew who I was, who everyone else was and what I had to do every day. In the classroom our teacher made daily attempts to draw us out, but unlike the señora Sara, he seemed to have a sense of when to insist and when not to. He knew a lot about our people but he said it was book learning, not real learning. He said the only thing you really knew for sure was what you had lived. I said that in that case, he was standing in front of a lot of very knowledgeable people. He smiled and said I was right. Then he closed his eyes, placed his arms across his chest and made a long, slow bow to us.

One day we were learning about numbers. I said they were real beings, just as important as days and seasons. "Take for example, the seven."

He looked at me puzzled. "Go on."

"The seven is the Time Being. It is in charge of time, so everything that there are seven of is also governed by time." I looked around the classroom, secretly proud of what I knew and at the same time embarrassed by my boldness.

He held a piece of chalk in one hand and nodded. "So, the numbers are gods, too."

"Yes." I looked around at my classmates. Did I dare say it? I took a deep breath. "Only I don't believe in the gods anymore."

Around me the class broke out in whispers.

He frowned. "You don't believe in numbers?"

All eyes stared at me, waiting for an answer. There was time to back down, but isn't that what we were learning—that we had the right to speak up? I met his glance. "In numbers, yes, but not in the gods."

He waited for an explanation.

"They left me. They left us—all of us. Why should I believe in them?"

He paced back and forth across the front of the classroom, rubbing his chin, then stopped in the middle, studied his feet and finally looked up at me. "They got you here, didn't they?"

His simple observation jolted me, planting within my mind the possibility that, up to this moment, all my conclusions had been wrong

The days at the mission were good. Perhaps the teacher was right. Maybe the gods had brought us to this safe haven. If that was the case, I intended to stay here. No sense in tempting them to change their minds about me.

Inside the mission everything was safe and predictable. Outside was a different story. Not a week went by that a new girl didn't come in, walking the thin line between living and dying, and undecided as to which to choose.

I volunteered to do lots of chores inside the mission so señora Sara wouldn't send me out on errands. Today I was making the rice. I soaked the rice and turned the tomatoes over the fire, roasting the skins so they'd be easier to peel. We didn't always have vegetables, and there was meat only once in a while, but rice we ate every day. Today I was making it with tomatoes, because yesterday it had been white. Another girl was working in the kitchen with me, chopping nopales.

"Will you show me how to make rice?" she asked.

I nodded. "It's easy. Just watch what I do." I drained the soaked rice and poured oil into a big earthenware casserole until it was about three fingers deep. While it heated I chopped two onions into nice little squares, the way I had learned, and mashed a couple of cloves of garlic. I could taste it already.

"Here's the molcajete," the girl said, putting the heavy mortar on the counter. Do you want me to mash the tomatoes?"

I glanced at the pile of nopales yet to dice. "Okay."

I fried the rice in the hot oil until it was golden, added the onion and garlic and let the mixture cook slightly before I drained the oil back into a can. Then I added the tomatoes, let them sizzle for a minute in the hot mixture and then added hot broth. Steam filled the kitchen. I made good rice. It was something I was proud of.

Twenty minutes later the señora Sara came in and told me it was my turn to go for tortillas. "But I'm cooking the rice," I said, shaking my head. "Can't you send someone else?"

"Micaela will go with you," the señora Sara said. She lifted the lid and peered into the earthenware pot. "Besides, the rice is done."

My fingers gripped the edge of the sink. "Why don't I just make the tortillas?" I asked. "I watched my grandmother. I know how."

She smiled and shook her head. "We don't have time to make that many tortillas." She reached into a drawer and pulled out two clean dishcloths. "You have to go out sooner or later. You can't stay here forever." She held out the dishcloths.

I disagreed with her. I could stay forever—until I got old and died. I never wanted to be anywhere else. I took the dishcloths and clutched them tightly, the way I would have liked to hold onto the mission and everybody in it.

She tugged playfully at the dishcloths "It's only a couple of blocks. You'll be fine. You'll see."

Why was she making me do something I wasn't ready for? "It's just that it's safe here," I pleaded.

She nodded. "I know," she said, touching her thumb to my cheek. "But I want to give you freedom."

Micaela and I opened the door and stood on the stoop. Once I had lived in the street and now I lived in fear of it. I looked out at the very place where I had, six months ago, stepped in front of a truck. I don't know what I was afraid of. Perhaps I was afraid of accidentally being hit by a truck, now that I wanted to live. Perhaps I feared wasting my life, now that I had it back. I don't know. Too many feelings clamored for attention. I couldn't sort any of them out. I clasped Micaela's hand in mine. "We'll be all right."

The señora pushed us out the door, the way she had pushed me out that day. Only this time she was laughing. "Go on, and hurry! We're all starving!"

The light on the street was blinding. The white concrete sidewalk and the dusty road reflected the bright daylight and magnified it. I gripped Micaela's hand and squinted as we walked two long and dusty blocks to the tortilleria. Each time a truck bolted down the hilly street the ground shook. I thought of the day I had walked in front of a truck. I shuddered. It would have hurt, dying like that. It would have hurt bad.

I walked next to the buildings, as far away from the street as I could. The line in front of the tortilleria snaked down the sidewalk. Micaela and I slipped into place at the end of it and stood, our eyes fixed on the ground. We waited. I counted the people in front of us. Twenty, then fifteen, then eleven, and then four.

There was something familiar about the boy at the front of the line. The way he held his shoulders, the shape of his head. He paid for his tortillas and turned to leave. I looked up and our eyes met. Without warning an embarrassing warmth filled my face, rushed through my body, tingled in my fingers. A sudden burst of sunshine radiated from my chest to my face and erupted in a huge smile that was impossible to hide. "Martín! Is it you? Is it really you?"

Was he all right? Did he remember me? Could we still be friends? So much had happened—did I dare hope he might still care? So many doubts clouded my mind only to vanish the moment he spoke.

He stopped. A broad grin broke out across his face. "I didn't know you were here."

We stood face to face, filling ourselves with each other. It was true. He was here, alive, and well. My first impulse was to reach out to him, to take his hand and hold on to it forever, but I paled at the thought of my own audacity. Instead I said, "I thought I had lost you."

He shook his head. "They shot me, but they didn't kill me." He looked down and shuffled his feet. "I couldn't die yet. I still owe you a rose."

"You're my rose." The words jumped out of my mouth. I don't know where they came from, but there they were, as raw as the moment. A slow burn crept across my face.

He grinned and looked up, tilting his head. "So, where are you staying?"

The words rolled off my tongue. "At the mission."

He shoved his hands into his pockets, the packet of tortillas pressed close to the side of his chest and the grin still on his face, and began to walk away, turning back to me as he spoke. "Then maybe I'll see you."

I nodded, too embarrassed and too happy to say anything. I watched him walk away, stop, turn around, and walk away again. The grin on his face just got bigger and bigger.

Somewhere a withered yellow kernel burst open and a tiny green cornstalk spiraled its way through the black earth. It reached upward to the blue sky and opened itself to the blazing sun.

Micaela and I reached the front of the line and it was our turn. What had started out as an important test had suddenly become nothing. The whole world had shifted. The gods had taken care of Martín and brought him back. Maybe the teacher was right. Maybe they had done the same for me. Maybe being wrong was the price of freedom. I looked at the woman and smiled as if buying tortillas were the most natural thing in the world for me. "Five kilos," I said, handing her our two cloths.

She put a stack of the warm corn cakes on her scale and weighed them, taking off and putting back on until the scales balanced.

"Micaela," I whispered. "You could have a job like this."

She smiled. "Do you think so?"

I put my hand on her shoulder. "You'd be good at it."

The woman put half on one cloth and half on the other, folded the towels around the stacks and handed one to each of us. I gave her the money and watched her count it and put it into her cash box. We lingered, watching her movements, dreaming of possibilities.

"Who's next?"

I turned away, pressing the warm bundle against my body. In my hands the corn god sprang to life. The earth shared her goodness, the sun rose victorious from the Underworld, and the tortillas were once again full of magic.

Chapter Nineteen

The days were growing colder and it was almost time to celebrate Muertos. We set up an altar in the classroom and each of us brought something that reminded us of someone we loved. I brought my red hair ribbons. They reminded me of my grandmother.

We covered the altar with a long yellow cloth, and then we set yellow candles into old bottles and spaced them evenly across the front. Some of the girls put toys for the spirits of babies that had gone to the Otherworld. The teacher brought three shiny brown loaves of pan de muertos, the special bread made at this time of the year, and the señora Sara came back from the market with a bunch of bright yellow marigolds, which we arranged in small glass jars. In the middle we placed a mound of copal resin in a clay burner and a sugar skull. It was a nice altar. I thought the spirits would be pleased.

The afternoon of the celebration the señora Sara called me into her office. I knocked on the glass door.

She looked up from a pile of papers and took off her glasses. "Come in, Rosa," she said, gesturing to a chair.

I sat down on the edge of the chair. "Have I done something wrong?"

She got up and came around to where I sat and leaned against the edge of the desk in front of me. "Not at all, quite the contrary." She reached out to smooth a stray lock of hair in my face. "You have made remarkable progress." She smiled. "You've learned to take care of yourself and your baby, you are quite good in the kitchen and you seem to have come to terms with the past. That's why I called you." She folded her arms in front of her. I think it's time for you to move on."

I didn't understand. I hoped she wasn't saying what I thought.

"I want you to start thinking about going home."

I clutched my stomach. No, no, she wasn't saying this. I was safe here. Life was good. I nodded and said "Yes, señora," the way I had been taught. I wanted to get down on my knees and beg. I'll do anything, only please, don't make me leave. I knew it was my fear speaking, but its voice was louder and more convincing than mine.

She must have read my mind. "You can't stay here forever." She smiled. "You can't let your fear speak for you. You have your own voice."

I wrapped my rebozo around me. "No, of course not, señora." Yes I can. Why can't I? I felt the panic settle in my stomach and then rise to my chest. I had to stay here. I would die anyplace else.

"I think it would be good for you to go home."

I nodded. "Yes, señora." Home? I couldn't go home. Home was where a father had sold his only daughter. The daughter he said he loved. Home was where I had failed in my responsibilities. Where I had spilled too much water and forgotten to feed the chickens. Home was where I had angered the gods. I couldn't go home.

She waited. "We all make mistakes."

I looked at the floor and shuffled my feet. Some mistakes were not to be forgiven. I cleared my throat. His mistakes and mine.

"Remember when your father needed your help?"

I nodded. It was my fault. If I hadn't angered the gods, they would have sent the rains and none of this would have happened. How could I tell my father that?

"It's not wrong to ask for help. It's the way we take care of ourselves." She sighed. "Sometimes we take care of others and sometimes others take care of us. It's a big circle. There's no shame in it."

I followed her with my eyes. You say that because you don't know everything.

She walked around to where I stood and put her hand on my shoulder. I loved the way her hand felt on my shoulder. It was safe and reassuring. Her words were what frightened me. She cupped my chin in her hand and looked into my eyes. "I want you to think about it. I'm not going to make you leave until you're ready."

She let go of my chin and put her arm around my shoulder as we walked to the door together. I would never go home, of that I was sure. I was also sure I didn't want to live in the street. So that only left one thing, but no one wanted an Indian girl with a baby. I was back where I started.

That night we gave the spirits a wonderful welcome. We gathered around the altar and lit the candles and incense and called in the people we loved. We told stories about them and watched the candles flicker when each one arrived. I think they liked meeting all of us and having their stories shared. It made them happy that we remembered them.

When I began to talk about my grandmother a big wind came and all the candles flickered.

"She must have been a great healer," Marisol said.

I nodded. "She was." I hesitated. I could feel everyone watching me, leaning in to hear what came next. "When my grandmother called the gods, they came in such a hurry, they nearly blew the candles out—just like tonight." I smiled to myself. "They really loved my grandmother." As I spoke, I couldn't help but wonder what they thought of me. Had they forgiven my angry outburst?

I didn't tell them how I used to sit in the hearts of the saints and ask to be a healer like my grandmother. It was such a long time ago. I wondered who was taking care of our people now that she was not there. Maybe no one. Maybe they were waiting for me.

After all the spirits had come and everyone had told their stories, we sang songs and talked until late in the night. We dipped pieces of pan de muerto into hot chocolate made with water and when our eyes wouldn't stay open any longer, we went to bed happy. I wrapped my beautiful baby girl, now plump and happy, in my arms and went to sleep.

My grandmother stood at the far end of the starry white road. I recognized her immediately, in spite of the great distance between us. Her soft, rounded body, the single long gray braid, the kindness and knowing that looked out of her eyes. She beckoned. I walked toward her, loving what flowed between us. I looked into her eyes. She knew. She knew everything, but she looked right past it, just like Saint John the Baptist. They must have been friends.

"Rosa," she said. "The sun feels no shame in his time in the Underworld. His only shame would be if he didn't fight the battle." She held her head to one side and smiled, the way she always did when she knew more than she was saying. "Reach into yourself and find your own truth. It's always been there."

I shook my head, disappointed. I didn't want to reach into myself. I knew what still lived there. What I wanted was to reach out to her and to find safety in her arms, feel the warmth of her body and rest my head against the sweetness of her heart. I reached out, but she began to back away.

I stood there on the starry road with outstretched arms, watching her recede into the great vastness. Then she was gone and the night sky glittered brilliantly around me, like a million mirrors showing me what I didn't want to see. My hands dropped to my sides, empty of their hoped-for embrace. I didn't want to reach inside. I knew what was there. I couldn't do it, no matter what she said, no matter what the spirits said. They didn't know what I had done.

The next afternoon Martín and I sat on the steps in front of the mission. He still wore old pants, but they were clean and not torn. The belt around his waist wasn't as loose as it had been. His hair was combed and there was no dirt on his face. He sat on the top step, his elbows resting on his knees.

"You must be getting paid on your job."

He nodded enthusiastically. "Guess what kind of work I do now."

I shook my head. "I don't know."

A big smile crossed his face. "I'm an albañil."

"A construction worker? Then you are learning to build." I remembered when I dreamed of being a healer like my grandmother. How out of reach it seemed now.

He nodded. The fire blazed in his eyes. "It's perfect, isn't it? I'm learning to build houses. Now I can build my own house and I can build houses for others, too."

I was happy for him. His life had meaning again. The gods were pleased with him. I didn't know what they thought about me.

"My house is going to have two rooms and a real roof."

I smiled. A bullet hadn't damaged his spirit at all. "Did it hurt when they shot you?"

He unbuttoned his shirt and pulled it open. "Do you want to see the scar?"

I leaned forward and looked. A round place the size of a fifty-peso coin lay just below his collarbone. The skin looked like it had gotten all jumbled up and tied itself into a knot. I winced. "It must have hurt a lot."

He grinned. "Not that much."

"I'm sorry they shot you."

He shrugged.

I studied my shoes for a moment. The gods had taken care of him. They had saved his life. Maybe they had forgiven me. "The señora says I should think about going home."

His face brightened. "That's a wonderful idea."

I shook my head. "I'm afraid."

"Of what?"

I thought for a moment. There were so many things I was afraid of. Of starving. Of living on the street. Of failing to take care of Flor. Of living with dishonor. Of dying the wrong way. Of hating my father. I looked at him. "Of everything."

He stared at the pebble in his hand. "Sometimes I'm afraid, too." Then he threw it in a high arc and watched it fall.

I studied his face. I didn't see any fear. I saw strength in his jaw, strength in his shoulders and determination in his eyes. I saw hands that were hardworking and a grip that was sure without grasping. I saw a boy who had survived a bullet and had come out the stronger for it. I saw a boy who could do anything. Everything was simple for him. But it wasn't that easy for me, and I didn't know if it ever would be. I stood up, feeling resentment churn in my stomach. "I have to go in now. It's my turn to help with supper." I walked inside and shut the door behind me.

Every day at the mission we learned something new. In the kitchen, in the classroom or in the talks we had in the afternoons. Sometimes we had to be pushed into our lessons and other times we embraced them with joy.

Unlike me, Flor progressed steadily toward her freedom. By the time the holidays approached she was walking with help. First she would stand impossibly on the tip of her big toe, then she'd let the rest of the toes touch the floor and would finally lower the rest of her foot. Having already decided where she wanted to go, she'd enlist the help of the nearest hand or piece of furniture to get there. Her determination was inspiring to us all. We laughed at her clumsy movements and marveled at how she made use of them.

At times frustration filled her face: when the hands beckoned instead of steadying or when the furniture was slightly out of reach. When she wanted to go on her own but was afraid to. At those times she mirrored my own indecision and lack of confidence. But unlike me, her hesitation quickly turned into determination and the clouded look on her face soon became joyful as she pushed forward and did the impossible.

She quickly grew fond of Martín and would run toward him, arms wide open. Just as she reached him she would fall forward into his arms, squealing with laughter. He'd swoop her up and pretend to toss her in the air and then both of them would laugh.

I watched, wishing I could be as free as they were. I couldn't help but think how ironic it was that my source of pain and shame was also the source of my greatest joy. Sometimes it seemed as if the gods were toying with me, putting two such opposite feelings into the same body.

I loved to watch Flor play with the other babies; I loved how she smelled, I loved the way her legs curved into her ankles, the smoothness of her skin, the way her big toe was so much fatter than the others, the sound of her voice when she laughed, the silly sounds that would someday be real words, the glow on her fat little cheeks and the spark of sunlight in her eyes. Those eyes held magic. The first time I looked deeply into them, their wisdom and infinite nature shocked me. I felt as though I had penetrated the realm of the gods themselves.

Martín rang the bell the next Friday. I sat out on the steps again, shivering in the weak December sun, my knees up under my chin. He sat next to me, leaning back on his elbows.

"They paid me today." He reached into his pocket and pulled out some bills. "See? I have money."

I was happy for him. "I'm glad." I was also envious. I had no money, no job, no anything. But then the gods loved him.

He took two bills out and separated them from the rest. "I'm going to spend these," he said, "and save the rest."

"For your house." I turned away from him, picked up a pebble and threw it as far as I could. I hated that house already. He had a house and I had nothing. My dreams had died and his were coming true.

He nodded. "For my house."

"It's good that you have a plan," I lied. I hated that he had a plan while I had none. How could I dare to dream of being a healer without the help of the gods? How could I approach the gods until I knew whether they had forgiven me?

"Do you want to go to the movies with me?"

I shrugged. "I don't know. What's it like?" Martín saw nothing of the battle going on inside me. It was just as well.

"There are seats that fold and you can buy popcorn and candy."

I laughed. "That sounds silly. What else?"

"People sit in the dark and watch the show on a big screen." He searched the ground for a pebble. "Sometimes the man puts his arm around the girl he is with."

His eyes searched for my eyes and his hand reached across the step and rested lightly on mine.

My whole body tensed.

Martín withdrew his hand and picked up another pebble.

I tried to think of something to say. "Do you remember when we first met? You bought me a drink at the street festival."

He smiled, held the pebble on its side and drew pictures in the dirt. "Yes."

"That was really nice of you."

He gave a muffled reply that only his knees and I could hear. "I liked you." The silence of the moment was eternal. Long after I had given up hope of hearing anything more he tossed the pebble and looked up. "I still do."

A thousand feelings rushed through me in a thousand directions. "I like you too." I looked down at my hand, pressed flat against the step. His hand rested on the same step, inches away. I took a deep breath, and moved my hand next to his.

He looked up and smiled. The world shifted once more, in an instant, just like that. It was beautiful again.

Micaela and I were getting bolder in our outings. Each week we ventured out a little farther. One day we went to the hardware store for a new clothesline, another time we went to a grocery that was four blocks away. The Christmas posadas would start in a couple of days and today we had gone all the way to the market to get some special treats for the piñata. It was a half-hour walk from the mission. We had bought a half-kilo of nuts and were picking out pieces of sugarcane when Micaela suddenly panicked.

She braced herself against the stall and clutched my skirt. "Let's go." Her face paled. "Please."

Still clasping the pieces of sugarcane, I turned to see what had upset her so.

Three boys walked down the narrow aisle toward us. "Hey, lookie, it's Micaela," one called.

All of a sudden they were all around us. One of them reached under the front of her rebozo. The other reached under her skirt. "Come on, Micaela, let's have a little fun. You liked it before, remember?" They taunted her, laughed, groped, moving from one place to another on her body. "Yeah, come on, Micaela, give us a little Christmas present."

She fought off their advances, screaming and thrashing her arms, but their hands rubbed, touched, and grabbed in spite of what she could do.

I froze. Fear filled my whole body. Suddenly I heard myself scream. "Get away! Leave her alone!"

My arms lashed out. I swung at the boys with the pieces of sugarcane. I hit the patrón. I hit the veins that stood out on his neck, I hit his smelly breath, hit his ignorance and his misery, his pettiness and his meanness.

I hit the priest for the part of him that did not practice the love he professed.

Out of nowhere my father's face appeared. "Why did you leave me?" I cried, bringing the cane down across his shoulder. "Why didn't you take care of me?" I sobbed hysterically. My worst regrets spilled out. The ones that had condemned me. "Why didn't you tell me not to anger the gods? I was just a child. I didn't know."

I thrashed, struck blow after blow, not seeing and not caring, only wanting to inflict punishment for my pain. "You should have told me!" I cried. "You should have protected me!" I swung out with the pieces of cane, bringing them down on any surface, soft or hard. "Why didn't you stop me that day? None of this would have happened if you had stopped me. I didn't understand about the gods. You should have told me!"

My father's face shone in a blue haze in front of my unseeing eyes. *There's nothing to forgive. They've loved you all the time.*

Suddenly the old women came out from behind their counters wielding brooms, which they swung at the boys. "Go on, get out of here!" they cried. "Leave these girls alone!" "Go on, get out!"

My father's face disappeared, and the boys, fending off blows now coming from everywhere, laughed. "Come on, let's get out of here," one said. They left, looking back and laughing as they sauntered along the narrow passageway.

I stood protectively over Micaela, gripping the pieces of sugarcane, tears streaming down my cheeks.

Two of the women put down their brooms and reached out to comfort us. The others returned to their counters, shaking their heads.

Micaela lay crumpled in a heap on the ground. One of the women sat down beside her and held her in her arms, murmuring softly in her ear and caressing her hair. Without thinking I threw my arms around the other woman and let the pain I had held back for so long run its course. My father's words encircled me, repeating themselves softly in my mind. *They've loved you all the time.*

That night at supper I looked around the table at the other girls who sat with me, dipping pieces of tortillas into bowls of hot soup and doubting, as I had, their right to exist. I wanted to stand up and shout, "The gods haven't left you! We misunderstood!" But I knew it was something each one had to discover for herself.

Each of us had to delve beyond the misunderstandings and find that

Chapter Twenty

"Flor, the gods have given us a splendid day."

My little girl, now thirteen months old, sat on the bed playing with a doll. Her eyes were bright, her cheeks glowed and her hair was neatly tied with ribbons. She looked up at me and smiled as if she agreed.

I looked out the window and took a deep breath. "Oh Flor, the sky is blue enough to get lost in," I said, glancing at her. Then turning back to the window, I continued, my arms flung open to embrace the fullness of what I sensed. "The mountains are so near—look—I can run my fingers across their ridges." I inhaled deeply. It was too full, too glorious, too wonderful to take in all at once. The air was so crisp, one breath at a time wasn't enough. I wanted to embrace the whole of creation, as if I were seeing it for the first time. It was a glorious new day and I was part of it.

I turned back to where Flor played, and slipped my blue blouse over my head. As I did, the whole sky settled lightly and I found myself again.

I picked up my skirt that was made from the wool of Saint John the Baptist and held it to my nose. I smelled the dark earth that it had come from; I felt the rocky hillside and saw my village down below. They were my foundation, my tradition, my people.

I reached for the belt I had woven on the backstrap loom with my grandmother's help. Once again it whispered her magic words. Slowly and carefully I wrapped it around me, understanding now that my body was the meeting place where heaven and earth joined together. I looked at Flor. "That's why we are the center of the universe. That's why we are important." I'd make sure she understood.

A knock on the door and Micaela entered. My grandmother had said that everything had a soul—a spark of the divine fire that burns in the sun. I could see that spark in Micaela. I knew that she would soon see it too.

"Do you want me to braid your hair?" she asked hesitantly.

I smiled and sat down in the little chair with my back to her. She took the comb and began to divide my hair for the braids.

I handed her a red ribbon. "Do you remember?"

She smiled shyly. "I think so."

I sat while she wove red ribbons into my hair. "Red is the color of the sun when it is just coming up over the horizon, Micaela. It's the color of life."

I watched in the mirror as she joined the two braids together at the bottom, the way we did in our village. It was what the Ancestors had taught since the beginning. The cycle was still alive and I was still part of it. I was who I had always been. Rosa. A gift from la Virgen.

Micaela finished and stepped back. "There."

I stood up and took her arm and we stood together in front of the mirror.

"In our village we grow flowers," I said, admiring our reflections. "Big, strong, beautiful flowers."

She blushed and lowered her gaze.

"Do you remember?" I asked.

She hung her head, as if she weren't sure which memories were safe and which were best avoided. "I don't know," she whispered.

I put my arms around her and held her close to me. "Micaela, the gods have always loved you," I said quietly.

She backed away as if she no longer knew who I was.

Flor sat on the bed, quietly watching. I opened the armoire door and took out the rebozo. Then I wrapped space and time around my shoulders and tucked her safely inside.

On the table stood a vase with a single white rose, the first of many. I held it to my nose for a moment and then I tucked it into my rebozo for my little girl.

I glanced back into the mirror, liking the girl I saw there. The gods had given us a splendid day. We were going home.

Epilogue

Martín insisted on carrying Flor on his back up the steep rocky trail to my village. When I said the men would make fun of him if they saw him doing woman's work, he laughed. I knew then that my parents would love him as much as Flor and I did. I reached out and took his hand, knowing that with so much love, everything would be all right.

My mother met us in the doorway. Her arms went from one to the other, trying to hold us each enough.

"And Papí?" I asked, when she finally ushered us inside.

She gestured with her chin toward the fields. "In the fields. Always in the fields." She held up her hands. "What can he possibly coax out of them at this time of year?" She sat down in the little chair by the comal with a deep sigh. "Your father sows his hopes and reaps his disappointments out there. The fields have become his life."

I left Flor with my mother and Martín and went to look for him. On the hillside above the village an elderly brown man, much thinner and more fragile than I remembered, bent over the sleeping winter dirt. "Papí," I called softly.

He stood up and turned around. He stared, and his hand let go of the dried stalks it clutched. Then his eyes filled with tears.

I reached out and put my arms around him. "Come, Papí. Let's go home."

The End

153

This story is based in part on fact.
Many thanks to the Rev. Delle McCormick
and the fates that arranged our chance meeting
on the streets of San Cristobal a few
summers ago.

Glossary

abuelita little grandmother
aguardiente firewater; homemade whiskey
albañil construction worker
autoridades village elders in charge of religious ceremonies
comal metal cooking surface
copal resin used as incense
chilaquiles dish made from dry tortillas and broth
chiles chili peppers
chiles rellenos stuffed chili peppers
Día de los Muertos Day of the Dead, November 1.
Día de los Santos Reyes Three Kings Day, January 6.
Doña a title of respect used with first names
elotes roasted corn on the cob
Flor Flower
frijoles beans
guavas guava fruit
hijita little daughter
la Virgen Virgin Mary, Mother of Jesus
masa dough for making tortillas
meztizos racial mix of Indian and Spanish
molcajete mortar for grinding spices and chilis
Muertos refers to Day of the Dead
niña little girl
niño little boy; the Christ child
nopales edible cactus paddles
paciencia patience
pan de muertos bread traditionally eaten on the Day of the Dead
Papá, Papí daddy
patrón, patrona boss (m,f.)
poblanos poblano chili peppers
poncho loose outer garment
posadas parties and parades held the nine days before Christmas, Dec 16-24.
¡Provecho! Enjoy your food!
rebozo shawl
Reyes Three Kings Day, January 6.
rosca ring cake eaten on January 6. A small plastic doll symbolizing the Christ child is baked inside.
señor, señora sir, ma'am; man, woman; Mr., Mrs.
shaman shaman; wise man or woman
tortillería tortilla store

International Organizations

Child abuse and child exploitation are worldwide problems, not just in Rosa's country. If you want to know more about organizations that are working to help solve them, you might take a look at the websites of the following:

Coalition Against Trafficking in Women
www.catwinternational.org

ECPAT International
www.ecpat.net

Equality Now
www.equalitynow.org

International Justice Mission
www.ijm.org

About the Author

Harriet Hamilton was a journalist, a writer, director and producer of prize-winning radio and television programs, and a teacher. She went to school in the United States, Paris, Frankfurt and Mexico and lived in Mexico for fifteen years. While she was there, she became aware of the abuse of children there and throughout the world and became interested in the groups who are helping to end that abuse. She considered herself a messenger to bring this problem to the attention of as many people as possible.

Ribbons of the Sun is her message.

Ribbons of the Sun was published posthumously. Harriet Hamilton died in January 2006, before its publication, although the manuscript was complete in every detail. We publish it with gratitude for her message and with pleasure for her graceful and moving story of Rosa's life.

THICK *by Colin Neenan*

Nick is a nice guy who wants to do the right thing.

But Nick has a problem. He has a lot of problems. He's slow in school, and he's bullied by a classmate. His father is an abusive drunk. And the girl he loves is being abused by her boyfriend.

But his worst problem has landed him in jail, awaiting trial.

Nick found a gun and accidentally shot someone.

THICK is an intense, suspenseful story for people who have a hard time finding a book they want to read.

They'll want to read this one.

THICK $6.95, higher in Canada
ISBN: 0974648191

At your booksellers or from the publisher.

Brown Barn Books
119 Kettle Creek Road
Weston, Connecticut 06883
editorial@brownbarnbooks.com